# HEAR NO EVIL

## Sudden Death

# HEAR NO EVIL

Death in the Afternoon
Missing!
A Time of Fear
Dead and Buried
Sudden Death

# HEAR NO EVIL

## Sudden Death

*Kate Chester*

SCHOLASTIC INC.
New York Toronto London Auckland Sydney

ISBN 0-590-87991-X

Copyright © 1997 by Dona Smith.
All rights reserved. Published by Scholastic Inc.
HEAR NO EVIL is a trademark of Scholastic Inc.

12 11 10 9 8 7 6 5 4 3 2 1          7 8 9/9 0 1 2/0

Printed in the U.S.A.                                      01

First Scholastic printing, February 1997

To the Reader:

Sara Howell is profoundly, postlingually deaf (meaning she lost her hearing after she learned to speak). She is fluent in American Sign Language (ASL), and English. She can read lips.

When a character speaks, quotation marks are used: "Watch out for that bus!" When a character signs, *italics* are used to indicate ASL: *Watch out for that bus!* Quotation marks and *italics* indicate the character is signing and speaking simultaneously: *"Watch out for that bus!"*

Unless the sign is described (for example: Sara circled her heart. *I'm sorry . . .* ), the italicized words are translations of ASL into English, not literal descriptions of the grammatical structure of American Sign Language.

# HEAR NO EVIL

## Sudden Death

# Chapter 1

It's so easy to catch some people in a lie, thought Sara. They said one thing with their mouths while everything else about them said something else. They didn't know that no matter what their lips said, their bodies whispered the truth. You only had to read the signs.

Sara was watching Amy Hendersen, the girl who sat across the aisle. She was fidgeting in her chair, and looking down at her hands. She'd been doing that ever since Liz Martinson announced she'd brought the pictures from her last party.

Amy pretended to be enthusiastic about seeing them, but Sara knew she was lying.

No matter what Amy said, Sara knew Amy didn't really want to see those pictures at all.

The bell rang, signaling the end of class. After gathering their books, Sara and Amy, along with their friends Keesha and Liz, pushed their way into Radley Academy's jam-packed hallway. It was lunchtime, and a tide of students, their heads bobbing up and down, flowed through the hall under the harsh glare of fluorescent ceiling lights.

Sara looked at Amy's strained expression and wondered why she didn't want to see the pictures. She certainly couldn't be worried that they weren't flattering. With her pale blond hair and violet eyes, Amy looked like an angel.

When Amy first transferred to Radley two months ago, everyone assumed she had a disposition to match her angelic looks. Amy proved them right, except when she came out with a wicked joke now and then, and laughed louder than anyone else.

Amy caught Sara's eye and she smiled, but her lips quivered a little at the corners. What is in those pictures that you don't want to see,

Amy? Sara asked her silently. She pushed a strand of long brown hair from her face.

The girls joined the throng of teenagers in green and white uniforms, jostling each other as they streamed into the cafeteria through open double doors. As one unit, she and her friends moved to their usual spot and tossed their books down carelessly on the long Formica table. For forty-five minutes, their time was their own.

The windows that stretched along one wall of the cafeteria rattled as rain splattered against them like a shower of pebbles. Outside the wind whipped through skeleton branches of the trees in a never-ending hiss. It was the kind of day that made you want to huddle close to a fire.

As Sara moved toward the crowded lunch line, Amy walked beside her, absently twisting a strand of pale blond hair. Her violet eyes had the blank, glassy look of someone who is in her own world.

Just as Sara picked up a tray, out of the corner of her eye she saw Amy heading right into the path of a worker carrying a bin of silverware. Amy didn't just bump him, she piled right into him, so hard that the silverware flew from his hands and cascaded to the floor. The small, round man stamped a foot and threw his hands in the air.

Amy stammered an apology and began picking up knives and forks. The man waved her away. As Amy joined Sara in the lunch line, she looked rattled, yet more in a fog than ever.

Sara slid her tray past the daily special — meat loaf — and nodded yes to the man who was serving the burgers. She grabbed an orange drink, and the two girls hurried to join their friends.

At identical tables all around, students swapped stories and exchanged confidences. Here and there couples stared into each other's eyes.

The air was full of the clinking noise of silverware against plates, laughter, and the steady hum of conversation. In one corner a group gyrated to the music from a portable CD player.

Sara Howell took in the color and movement, but she couldn't hear the sounds. Sara was deaf.

For the first six years of her life, Sara had been a hearing person. Then, in spring, a case of meningitis left her wrapped forever in a cloak of silence. Now she communicated by using American Sign Language, and by lip-reading, and speaking.

Sara sat down and began pouring ketchup onto her burger as she scanned the cafeteria. Suddenly she felt as if she was fading, fading, until she was invisible and alone in the crowded room. The sensation hit her without warning and with all the force of a punch in the gut. She signed to herself in her thoughts, *DIFFERENT, DEAF. DIFFERENT, DEAF.*

The other girls at the table went on talking and laughing. Sara looked at them and felt far away. She took a deep breath. Will this ever stop happening? she asked herself.

Sara's best friend Keesha Fletcher tapped her on the arm, and the feeling vanished. Sara felt herself returning as if she had been swimming underwater and suddenly burst through to the surface. As Keesha's fingers began to move, Sara gave a silent prayer of thanks for Keesha's fluency in American Sign Language.

*Pictures. Party. Look,* Keesha signed. She reached toward a stack of photos on the table. Next to her, red-headed Liz Martinson smiled and nodded.

Sara saw Amy bite her lip. She stretched her hand out and rested it on top of the stack of pictures. She said something to Keesha, her smile growing brighter and brighter.

Too bright, thought Sara. It isn't real. She knew, with the sixth sense she had developed, that Amy had said something about her. She felt a prickle of irritation. One of the most annoying things about being deaf was having hearing people talk about you as if you were on another planet, when you were sitting right there.

Sara started to interrupt angrily, to tell Amy — talk to me, you know I can read lips. She stopped herself. Amy had never done that before. But then, Amy wasn't herself today.

Keesha shot Sara an apologetic glance, then looked at Amy and wrapped her first three fingers over her thumb to sign *M.* Keesha pushed her fist forward twice to sign *M.M.*

Sara recognized the shorthand for *minor miracle,* their term for anything Sara's brother agreed to without a struggle.

Keesha turned to Sara and started signing. *Amy is amazed that your brother let you go to the party when he was out of town. I told her it was a minor miracle and taught her our sign.*

Sara touched her fist to her forehead and flicked her index finger upward. *Understand.*

At 22, Sara's brother, Detective Steve Howell, was her legal guardian. He wanted so much to prove he could handle the responsibility that he went overboard at times. It created tangles in their relationship.

When Sara lost her hearing she had gone to board at the Edgewood School for the Deaf. Since then she had only spent summer vacations at home with her brother. But last August, everything changed. A hit-and-run driver had taken her beloved father from her and turned her world upside down. She had returned to Radley, to a hearing environment and a hearing school, to live with a brother she did not know well.

Tragedy had forged a deep and instant bond between them. Now they only had each other, but the relationship was full of difficulty as well as closeness. Steve had trouble understanding Sara's muffled speech. Sara couldn't always read his lips, and his signing was awkward and difficult to understand. On top of it all, Steve felt he had to be the perfect father figure at all times. Still, their love for each other got them through the rough spots and brought them closer and closer together.

Amy took her hand off the pile of pictures and picked up her sandwich. Keesha picked a photo off the top of the pile and held up a picture of Amy dancing with Wayne Hansen. The second photo she held up was also of Amy and Wayne.

Keesha slid the pictures across the table to Sara. In both shots, the camera had caught the dancing couple mirroring each other's movements, smiling into each other's faces.

Amy stiffened. Her violet eyes grew wide. "There is nothing going on between Wayne and me," she blurted.

Her lips formed a tight little smile. She tapped the pictures and looked at Sara. *"Mark would be jealous,"* she signed as she spoke. Amy flipped her fist with outstretched pinkie away from her mouth. *Jealous.*

Amy was picking up more ASL signs every day. One of the first she had learned was *jealous.* As she signed the words her lips parted in a forced laugh, as if to say, I'm only kidding.

*Understand.* Sara tapped her forehead and raised her index finger. You're not kidding, Amy, she thought.

Keesha gave a dismissive wave of her hand. She tapped Sara on the arm and pointed to a photo. She held up a picture of Sara and her boyfriend Bret standing arm in arm.

Amy nudged Sara. "Maybe you and Bret can double-date with Mark and me sometime," she said.

"Sure." Sara didn't want to hurt Amy's feelings, but she didn't think she'd ever want to double-date with them. Mark was sometimes hard to take. She hoped that Amy couldn't read her thoughts.

Sara had seen the way Amy tensed up

when Mark was in one of his moods. She could tell when Amy was being extra careful not to say the wrong thing. She had watched Amy break off conversations with guys whenever she saw Mark, even if they were only talking about homework. Just thinking about it made Sara's blood simmer.

When Sara saw Amy slide the photos under her cafeteria tray, she knew that Mark would show up any minute. Things must be even worse than she thought if Amy had to hide the pictures from him. She was beginning to get the feeling that Amy was afraid of Mark.

Before Amy could say any more about double-dating, Sara changed the subject to the history project she and Amy were working on. "Are we still getting together after school?" she asked.

Amy gave a brief nod, but her eyes were elsewhere. She smoothed her pale hair and sat up straighter. She looked like an actress getting ready to go onstage.

Sara followed Amy's line of vision. Mark Royce, Amy's boyfriend, was approaching with two friends at his side. Their steps were out of synch — for every step Mark took, the other boys took two. Mark's broad shoulders strained against the fabric of the white Radley Academy shirt that outlined the muscles of his chest. He swung several books easily in one large hand. A lock of dark, wavy hair fell casually over his forehead.

At six feet two and 220 pounds, Mark Royce was one of the biggest guys in school. Sara knew the athletic department was always after him to join one of the teams, but Mark had no time for sports. After school he helped out in his dad's warehouse. The tough, physical work had given him the hard muscles of an athlete.

Mark didn't take his eyes off Amy and as he came toward her he smiled broadly, revealing a chipped front tooth. When he reached the table, Mark kissed Amy lightly on the forehead. Then he nodded to the others and sat down, turning his back toward them as if to shut them out. The other two guys left and soon Mark and Amy were deep in conversation.

Sara moved closer to Keesha and Liz. She saw her two friends cast sidelong glances at Mark. The three of them looked at each other in silence for a moment, communicating their agreement that none of them cared for Mark Royce.

The girls began talking, but Sara would never recall what the conversation was about. She would only remember that after a moment she asked a question, and Liz and Keesha didn't answer. They weren't looking at Sara anymore. Their eyes had turned to the end of the table.

Sara's dark eyes took in the scene. Mark was standing over Amy, his features clouded with anger. A vein throbbed at his temple.

Mark was holding a photograph and waving it at Amy. He jabbed a thick index finger at her as he spoke.

Sara tried to read Mark's lips, but he kept bending down to put his face close to Amy's, then standing up and twisting around. She only caught a few words here and there . . . "dating" . . . "flirting" . . . "thoughtless."

She put her hand on Keesha's arm. When

Keesha turned to face her she signed, *What's going on? What are they fighting about?*

Sara read the concern on Keesha's face as her friend signed back rapidly, *Mark spotted the pictures of Amy dancing with Wayne Hansen, and got really angry. He accused Amy of dating Wayne and flirting with other guys. He says she's thoughtless to do it when he's under so much pressure.*

Sara signed back. *What's wrong with him? Amy isn't dating anybody else. He's crazy.*

Keesha nodded. *That's what Amy says, but Mark doesn't believe her.*

Suddenly Amy jumped up from the table, grabbed her books, and ran from the cafeteria. Now Sara would see Mark's face clearly. She was shocked at the rage she saw there.

Mark sprung to his feet. His chair slid backward and fell.

"Hey!" grunted a boy who was walking past as the chair struck him in the leg.

Mark whipped around and faced the boy, his teeth clenched and his hands balled into fists.

The boy held up both hands and backed away without saying a word.

Mark whirled back around and pointed at Amy's retreating form. Sara read his lips as he shouted after Amy, "You'll be sorry."

He stood there, still and silent, a dark angry shadow, until Amy disappeared.

## Chapter 2

All eyes were on Mark. Suddenly, he exploded into action. He pounded his fist on the table. Then in one furious motion he sent Amy's lunch tray crashing against the wall.

Soup splashed against the tile and dishes and utensils flew into the air. People jumped away to avoid being splattered.

Monitors came running from both ends of the cafeteria. "Stay away from me," Mark yelled to the two boys as they approached.

The monitors did as they were told and stopped in their tracks. Nobody in school wanted to tangle with Mark Royce, especially when he was angry.

There was a tension-filled stillness in the air. Then Wayne Hansen got up and started toward Mark. He wasn't nearly as tall as Mark, but his body was compact and power-fully built. He moved with a combination of confidence and caution. His walk was the muscle-bound gait of a wrestler.

Sara could read Wayne's lips as he said, "Take it easy, Royce."

"You're the last person I want to hear from right now," Mark snapped. "And another thing. Stay away from my girlfriend."

Wayne kept moving toward Mark. "You've got it all wrong. There is nothing between me and Amy."

Mark clenched and unclenched his fists. Beads of sweat had broken out on his fore-head. From the way he moved his mouth, Sara knew he was yelling. She caught the words, "lying . . . pictures . . . no fool."

Wayne stepped in front of Mark. Sara couldn't see his face anymore. She signed to Keesha. *What are they saying now?*

Keesha signed back. *Nothing.*

In a powerful lunge, Mark turned and hurled himself at Wayne. Students gasped and stared open-mouthed as his arm snapped back and he sent a huge fist smashing into Wayne's jaw.

Wayne staggered and was sent sprawling backwards against some cafeteria chairs. Students jostled each other as they hurried to get out of the way.

Wayne pushed himself up and threw himself at Mark, slamming into him and sending him thudding to the floor. He jumped into a crouch over Mark's body and threw a punch toward his face.

It never connected. Wayne was still for a moment, his fist pulled back, sucking in air. Time hung suspended as everyone waited, tense and breathless, to see what would happen. Then Wayne stood up so slowly it looked as if he was fighting against an invisible hand that pulled his collar. He touched his bleeding lip and glanced at the blood on his fingers.

"Okay, Royce, that's enough," he panted. "Let's just end this right now." With a defiant glance he turned his back and walked away.

Mark pushed himself to his feet. He stood staring after Wayne, his body shaking with rage. The air was heavy with silence.

After a moment Mark squared his shoulders and stalked out of the cafeteria. Students moved aside and made a wide path for him.

As soon as Mark was gone, the room began buzzing as everybody started talking at once. Keesha's fingers flew as she signed. *Did you see that? Mark was out of control.*

Sara nodded, and signed back, *It's hard to believe that a few pictures of Amy dancing with someone else would set him off like that.* It didn't feel right to her. *It's weird.* She moved her hand in an arc in front of her face.

Keesha signed back in agreement, *Weird.*

For the rest of the afternoon Sara's thoughts kept turning to Amy. Why did she put up with Mark Royce?

When Amy first came to Radley Academy, her fragile beauty and friendly, mischievous personality caught the attention of lots of boys. None had pursued her as strongly as Mark Royce. He made it no secret that he wanted Amy and he didn't want to share her with any other guy.

Did Mark's single-minded interest in her make Amy feel more secure? Sara wondered. Was he an anchor in a sea of new faces?

She thought back to her first few weeks at Radley, after going to the Edgewood School for the Deaf. She had always felt a little lost, a bit off-balance. Her longtime friends Keesha and Liz had been there for her when she was thrust into the hearing world.

Her boyfriend, Bret Sanderson, had been a great help too. Bret was fluent with ASL, because his parents were deaf. Although he went to another school, Sara could always count on Bret to understand, and on his warm embrace. Bret didn't have fits of temper. Bret didn't make people afraid.

A dark curtain fell over Sara's thoughts. Mark Royce wasn't understanding. There was no comparison between Bret and Mark. Sara was left with her original question — why did Amy put up with Mark?

She felt a tap on her arm and looked into the frowning face of her interpreter, Suzanne Andrews. Even before Ms. Andrews signed *pay attention,* Sara knew she had been caught daydreaming. Her interpreter accompanied her to nearly every class, signing so that Sara could follow what the teacher said. Hours of sitting next to Sara in class had taught Ms.

Andrews to recognize when she was day-dreaming.

Sara forced herself to focus as Ms. Andrews signed the teacher's words. She found it was a relief to take a break from her troubling thoughts.

After class, Sara searched for Amy in the crowded hallway. When she finally saw Amy pass by, with Mark at her side, it didn't look as if she wanted him there. Mark was bending down, speaking into her ear. Amy kept shaking her head. Sara could tell from the redness in her eyes that she had been crying. She caught the words "leave me alone" on Amy's lips as the couple passed by.

When Amy didn't show up in history class, Sara kept stealing glances at her empty chair. It wasn't like Amy to cut class.

She was relieved to see Amy waiting by her locker at the end of the school day. Her eyes were swollen and redder than before; her pale blond hair was disheveled and her face was ashen.

"Where were you, Amy?"

Sara watched Amy let out a sigh. "I went

for a walk. Then I sat in a coffee shop and wrote in my diary."

Amy didn't have to explain anymore. Sara could tell how upset she was.

Amy doesn't need to write about the situation in her diary, Sara thought. She needs to do something about it.

She touched Amy's shoulder gently, and then spoke. "Does Mark's temper ever frighten you?" Instead of spelling out Mark's name she used the name sign she and Amy had created for him — M plus the sign for strong.

Amy brushed a strand of blond hair from her forehead. "No. I know why he's been flying off the handle lately."

Sara watched Amy's lips as she explained that Mark wanted desperately to go to college, but his family couldn't afford to send him. "He's under a lot of pressure."

Sara knitted her brows and signed, *Pressure?*

Amy looked at her quizzically. "It's because of the scholarship exam."

Sara looked at her blankly.

"The Radley Business Association Scholarship," Amy explained. "The exam is coming up this week."

Sara shrugged. She didn't know anything about the exam.

Amy gave her head a little shake. After a moment, understanding dawned on her face. "I guess I've heard so much about it from Mark lately that I thought everybody knew. It's a four-year college scholarship for a student from Radley who wants to major in business."

Sara nodded, and Amy continued explaining, with Sara motioning for her to slow down the torrent of words every so often.

To be eligible for the scholarship a student had to have high grades, and submit a long application. If he or she qualified, an exam prepared by the Business Association was the next step. Whoever scored highest on the exam got the scholarship.

Mark was determined to win it. He was obsessed. Amy said he'd been so wound up during the past couple of weeks that he was ready to explode.

He did explode, Sara thought, reflecting on

his behavior at lunchtime. Looking at Amy, she felt as if a shadow had fallen upon her.

"What Mark really needs is a scholarship to charm school," Amy said, trying to make one of her usual jokes. It seemed forced, and fell flat, making the situation even darker.

Amy must have seen the look of doubt on Sara's face. "I know you don't like the way Mark acts sometimes, but I know a different side of him." A dreamy look appeared in Amy's eyes. "He's not the tough guy he wants everyone to think he is. When we're alone he doesn't have to pretend."

For a moment Sara wanted to shake her and shout, "Come to your senses!"

She knew it would be useless. Mark was making Amy miserable, but she was convinced that there was something wonderful about him that only she could reach.

"Let's go work on the history project," Amy said.

Sara raised her eyebrows. It didn't look as if Amy was capable of concentrating on anything. Then again, she thought, working on the project might take Amy's mind off her problems for a while. Perhaps afterwards she would see things more clearly.

Sara looked at the pile of books in Amy's arms. "Sure you're not forgetting anything?" she asked teasing.

The last time they had gotten together to study, Amy had left the notebook with all her notes on the project at school. They had gotten halfway to her house before she realized it and turned back.

Amy managed a smile. "I left the notebook at home. That way I couldn't possibly forget it."

Sara touched her right index finger to her forehead, then pointed forward. *Smart.* She pulled her coat on and closed her locker. The girls began walking toward the gym. Going through it was the quickest way to get to the parking lot.

A handful of basketball players were practicing layup shots. Sara looked at them and thought of her boyfriend, Bret. He played basketball for Radley's rival, Penham School. Thank goodness he's nothing like Mark Royce, she thought.

Sara pushed open the door and the two girls stepped into the late afternoon chill. "My car is over there," Amy said, motioning to a corner of the parking lot.

Sara looked in that direction, and then both girls gasped, surprised by what they saw. A crowd had gathered at the edge of the parking lot. Club meetings and sports practices were ending, and more students drifted over.

Sara and Amy hurried to see what everyone was looking at. The two girls broke through the crowd and stopped dead in their tracks. Someone had taken a baseball bat to Amy's car. The windshield, the windows, the headlights and taillights were smashed. Huge dents had been pounded into the hood, the roof, the doors, and the fenders. All four tires had been slashed.

They didn't stop there. They had opened the hood and continued to batter the engine.

Sara's stomach gave a sickening lurch. She looked from Amy's drawn, pale face to the battered shell of her car. Both Wayne and Mark were among the crowd of onlookers.

They stood apart, but Sara saw them exchange dark, electric glances. There was a jagged rip in the sleeve of Mark's jacket.

The ground seemed to tilt under her feet. Sara looked from Mark, to Wayne, and then to Amy. She sensed something lurking beneath the surface, something dark and twisted. She was afraid for Amy.

## Chapter 3

"My car," Amy's lips moved as if she were in a trance. Her eyes were glazed with disbelief.

Then, as Amy snapped back to reality, her features crumpled in horror. She raised a hand to her mouth and closed her eyes.

When Amy opened her eyes, everything looked the same as before. She had hoped the sight would go away.

From the edge of the crowd, Mark started toward Amy, his face set with determination. At the same time, Wayne began moving toward her.

Mark got there first, and Wayne hesitated, watching and waiting. Sara remembered how Amy had blurted out that there was nothing between her and Wayne. She wasn't convinced.

Amy reached out with both hands and pushed against Mark's chest, hard. He didn't budge, didn't look as if he'd felt a thing. He moved closer and started talking to Amy. The two exchanged words that Sara couldn't read.

Sara could see that the skin on Mark's knuckles was torn and flecked with blood. That didn't come from hitting Wayne, she thought.

Mark and Amy finished talking and Mark walked away. As he did, he stared hard at Wayne, daring him to get near Amy. Wayne didn't move, and as Mark passed him on the way back to the school building, he stopped and their eyes locked. After a long moment, Wayne turned and walked away, with Mark close behind.

Amy faced the gawking crowd and shouted something. Sara watched as people shook their heads. Here and there people mumbled, "No."

Sara filled in the blanks and understood that no one had witnessed what had happened. Either that, or no one had nerve enough to admit it. She had a pretty good idea who was responsible, though, and she thought that everyone else did, too.

After a few awkward moments the crowd began to break apart. There were words of whispered sympathy for Amy.

"Do you have any idea who did this, Amy?" Sara asked.

Amy looked away. She looked back at Sara's face, but not into her eyes. "No."

"You must have some idea," Sara prompted.

Again there was the furtive sidelong glance. Once again, Amy's lips said "No," but she didn't look Sara in the eye.

The blood churned in Sara's veins. "Mark!" She spat out the name.

Amy's head jerked up. "That's not true! It wasn't Mark," she said with such force that Sara took a step back. Her breath caught in her throat.

Amy looked away again, and mumbled something Sara couldn't understand. She put her hands on Amy's shoulders.

"Say again. Look at me."

Amy twisted her hands. She drew a line in the gravel of the parking lot with her toe. "The other day when we came back to school and I ran inside to get my notebook, I found something out. Something important. That's why my car was trashed."

"What did you find out?"

"I can't tell you."

Sara signed as she spoke, jabbing the air. *"You've got to tell me, Amy. This looks dangerous."*

"I just can't," Amy said, and pressed her lips into a thin line.

Sara threw her hands in the air. I can't help you if you won't tell me what the problem is, she thought with exasperation.

Amy folded her arms across her chest and stared at the ground.

Sara looked at her standing there, stiff and still. Questions tumbled over each other in her mind. What is Amy hiding? Why? How does Wayne fit in to this?

Amy smoothed her hair and looked up at Sara with wide, innocent eyes. "Never mind what I said about finding something out," she said. "It wasn't true." Her mouth curved into a half smile. "I just made it up, that's all."

As Sara stared in surprise, Amy gave a little shrug. "I don't know who did this to my car. Really. I don't think Mark would do this."

Yes, you do, Amy, Sara thought as she watched a dull red flush flow from Amy's collar until it had flooded her face. She thought she understood what Amy had done. She had made up her mysterious story to protect Mark, and then couldn't go through with the lie. The biggest lie was the one Amy was telling herself about Mark, she thought.

Sara felt hot sparks of anger. If you want to let Mark trash your car and do nothing about it, that's your business, Amy, she said to herself.

With a jerk of her head toward her green sedan, Sara turned and started walking briskly, her hands stuffed in her pockets. Amy followed slowly, her shoulders hunched.

Sara didn't usually take her car to school since Thurston Court was only a few blocks away. Today, however, she planned to go to

Amy's house, high up on the ridge overlooking the Buckeye River. Amy lived in Winchester Commons, home to some of the wealthiest people in Radley.

As Sara put the key in the ignition, Amy put a hand on her arm. Sara turned so that she could read her lips. "Wait. Don't be angry. I just can't work on the project now. Too much has happened . . ." Amy shrugged helplessly. She drew a circle around her heart. *Sorry.*

Sara's anger drained away and she felt suddenly tired. She drummed her fingers on the steering wheel. "Go home?" She searched Amy's face, wishing she could tell what was going on inside her head.

"Would you mind dropping me off at the Radley Library? I'm supposed to meet Mark there later."

Amy's words sent a shock through Sara. She raised her eyebrows in astonishment. "Amy!" she blurted.

Amy twisted her hair, her eyes blank. "Mark wants to talk. I'm sure he wants to apologize."

Sara watched the words form on Amy's

lips. She remembered how Mark had looked in the cafeteria that day, like some kind of raging animal.

Amy folded her arms. "I'm going to give him a chance. He needs me now."

Sara tried to push away the queasy feeling that was building into panic. She saw the look of defiance in Amy's eyes.

*Okay,* she signed with resignation. She pulled out of the parking lot and turned in the opposite direction from Buckeye Ridge, toward the downtown section of Radley.

As they rode Sara glanced at Amy. It looked as if she was carrying a heavy burden inside.

Strange, thought Sara, that sometimes people who had the most money were also the most unhappy. Her friend Kimberly Roth also lived in Winchester Commons. Her family was wealthy, but Kim had made a lot of money herself, working as a model. Right now she was at a shoot in Jamaica. Her life seemed full of excitement and glamour, yet Kim was one of the loneliest people Sara knew.

When the Radley Free Library was in sight, Sara looked at it through a veil of dread. The building, flanked by globed lamps, stood on the park in Penn Square and usually gave her a warm feeling. She loved the solid brick structure with its wood and brass interior. She would never forget that it was where she had met her boyfriend Bret.

Today, however, nothing could banish the chill that had settled in her heart. "Good luck talking to Mark, Amy," Sara said as Amy got out of the car. It wasn't what she wanted to say at all, but she knew no words would convince Amy not to see Mark. As an afterthought she added, "Be careful."

She watched as Amy ran up the steps to the library. Sara had a final glimpse of Amy's blond hair swaying as she disappeared inside.

Resolutely, Sara pressed her foot on the gas pedal and eased the car away from the library. She continued down Penn Street, and past the fourth precinct, where Steve was a detective. People were beginning to head home from work, and traffic was thickening.

Suddenly, the brake lights of the station wagon up ahead blazed in her eyes. Sara jammed on her own brakes. The force of the sudden stop jerked her forward in her seat. Her ribs hit the steering wheel painfully, knocking the wind out of her.

The driver ahead turned around and looked at her with frightened, angry eyes. Above them the stoplight glowed red.

*I wasn't paying attention. I was preoccupied with what's going on with Amy,* Sara thought with a combination of guilt and fear. *I nearly rear ended that car. I almost caused a serious accident.*

Trembling, she pulled the car over in front of the Penn Street Deli. She'd decided to get out of the car for a few minutes, and figured she might as well pick up something for dinner. She sat in the car until she was sure she could stand.

Sara entered the store slowly. The near miss had left her legs feeling like jelly.

She inhaled the rich aromas of salami, cheese, and the Italian specialties the Patrone family prepared daily. She decided to get the lasagna, and wrote the order on a piece of paper from the small spiral notebook she kept in her purse.

Grandfatherly Emilio Patrone smiled as he took Sara's order. "It's good to see you, Sara. Why have you stayed away so long?"

Sara smiled and shrugged. "Busy." She didn't want to tell Emilio the real reason she hadn't stopped by sooner. Ever since her father died, the Patrones had insisted on giving Sara and her brother whatever they ordered free of charge. It made Sara feel good that they wanted to be kind, but it embarrassed her, too.

Mr. Patrone bagged her order and waved away the bills she held out, as she had known he would. Sara could feel herself blushing as she took the bag from his hands and left the store.

When Sara entered the apartment, she was greeted by Tuck, the golden retriever that was her hearing ear dog. She ruffled his fur, and then went to stash the lasagna in the refrigerator.

Her eyes rested on the folded piece of

paper in the middle of the table. Before she picked it up she was sure it was a note from Steve, and her heart sank. She already knew what it said. Tuck brushed against her legs as she read her brother's familiar scrawl:

> Sara,
> I have to work late again. I won't be home for dinner. Don't wait up for me. Sorry.
>
> Steve

Sara let the note fall from her fingers. Steve often worked late, but Sara never got used to it. She especially hated having dinner alone, sitting at the dining room table.

During most months, Sara spent several afternoons practicing with the Radley Academy Crew Team. She loved the beauty of the sight of the rowing shells skimming the water. She loved the power of the oars in her hands and the soaring, free feeling rowing gave her.

Now, however, it was too cold for crew practice. Sara was left with more time on her hands — more time to be by herself in the apartment.

Although she knew it wasn't Steve's fault that he had to work late, Sara felt a ripple of anger. She decided she wasn't going to spend another minute in the apartment. Sara walked quickly to the kitchen and spooned some food from a can into Tuck's dish. Then she went across the hall and knocked on Keesha's door. She suddenly felt an overwhelming need to talk to her.

She and Keesha had been best friends since the Fletchers moved in across the hall when the girls were five. After Sara lost her hearing, Keesha had studied ASL with her. The girls created name signs for each other. *K* plus linked fingers, the sign for *friend,* meant Keesha. *S* plus *friend* meant Sara. Together they had created the name sign *L-RED* for their red-haired friend, Liz. Recently, they'd made up a sign for violet-eyed Amy: *A-VIOLET.*

As Sara stood at the door, she conjured up a picture of Keesha's dark features. The difference in their color had never made a difference in the way they felt about each other. They could practically read each other's thoughts sometimes. Sara hoped that Keesha would be able to help her sort things out.

Keesha's mother answered. As soon as Sara saw Brenda Fletcher's face, with its welcoming smile, her heart felt lighter.

The Fletchers treated her like family. Mrs. Fletcher was head of Radley Academy's lower school, where the younger children attended. She had helped Sara get the financial aid she needed to afford private school, and even found her an interpreter.

Mrs. Fletcher motioned her inside. Sara walked past the alcove where rows of children's books stood on shelves, and into the living room.

Keesha was lying on the couch reading a magazine. When she saw Sara she sat up, her eyes widening with surprise. *I thought you were studying with Amy,* she signed.

*We were supposed to study, but Amy was too upset.* Sara signed as she sat down. *Her car was trashed. It was awful. The tires were slashed, the windows smashed in, dents all over it.*

Keesha's jaw dropped. *Do you think Mark did it?*

Sara nodded. *Yes. Amy insists he wouldn't. She's going to meet him later.*

Keesha slapped her thigh. *Common sense, girl!* she signed. It was one of her favorite expressions. Sara thought Amy could use a dose of it. When it came to Mark she just couldn't seem to think clearly.

Sara ran her hands through her long brown hair. *I'm worried about her.*

A line creased Keesha's forehead. *Me, too.*

Sara stayed at the Fletchers' apartment for dinner. By the end of the meal with Keesha and her parents in the cheerful, cozy dining room, the feelings of sadness had faded.

But when Sara returned to her empty apartment, it all came rushing back. The dark rooms were draped in shadows. The sight chilled Sara inside. She walked through, turning on lamps along the way. She always felt better when she was alone if the apartment was blazing with light.

Sara never told Steve how she felt about

being alone after dark. She couldn't quite understand it, and didn't even like to admit it to herself. It didn't fit with the rest of her.

Sara sat down at her desk and forced herself to concentrate on her homework. At around ten o'clock, Bret called her on the TTY, the telecommunications machine that augmented the telephone. Warmth surged through her as she saw the words, **I miss you.**

**I miss you, too,** she typed. Then she told him what had happened that day, and how afraid she was for Amy.

Bret's reply wasn't exactly what she expected. **Don't get involved. Don't get in this guy's way. You always end up in the middle of a dangerous situation.** She thought he would tell her he agreed about Mark's temper, or say that Amy should have more sense, the way Keesha did.

The more she tried to talk about Amy, the shorter Bret's answers became. In the end, Sara had to drop the subject. Bret didn't want to hear about it.

Sara signed off the TTY feeling disappointed. She missed being able to confide in Bret the way she usually did. Tonight he had seemed so different.

Sara took Tuck out for a short walk, and then got ready for bed. Steve had not returned home by the time she drifted off to sleep.

When Sara's bedside lamp flashed to wake her up for school the next morning, Steve still had not returned home. The light that came in the kitchen window was pearly as she fixed herself a quick breakfast of cereal and coffee. She found that she couldn't eat more than a mouthful. Her stomach was tied up in knots.

She didn't feel any better when she called Steve on the TTY and there was no answer in his office. Steve had worked all night before, but this time something felt different — wrong.

When Sara got to school Amy wasn't waiting at her locker as she usually did, to talk before homeroom. When she didn't come to second-period biology, the knots in Sara's stomach tightened. Through the classroom window, she could see the wreckage of Amy's car still sitting in the school parking lot. It was an eerie signal that Amy hadn't gotten the car towed to a garage. It wasn't like Amy to neglect such things, Sara thought as she averted her eyes.

After class she waited while Keesha dialed the number at Amy's house from the pay phone in the hall. She watched as Keesha's features tightened. *What's wrong?* she signed frantically as soon as Keesha hung up the phone.

*The maid answered. She said Amy wasn't there. When I asked her where she went, the maid hung up on me.*

*This feels strange,* she signed to Keesha.

Fear showed on Keesha's face, but she signed, *Calm down. Let's not jump to conclusions.*

At lunchtime, Sara, Keesha, and Liz met at the table they shared with Amy. Nobody ate much. They spent the time trying to convince themselves, and each other, that there was nothing to worry about — Amy would arrive at school later that afternoon, or the next day. They went through the motions of talking about other things, trying to pretend that they could think of something besides Amy.

*Call Amy's house again,* Sara signed to Keesha when they passed the pay phone after lunch. Keesha hesitated a moment, then nodded.

Sara watched Keesha drop the quarter into the slot and dial. She didn't take her eyes from Keesha's face as she waited, and waited . . . and waited. *No answer,* Keesha signed finally, her head tilted to cradle the phone against her shoulder. The two girls looked into each other's eyes, both reading dark thoughts.

Keesha turned to hang up, then stopped suddenly. Sara watched the skin on her knuckles tighten as she gripped the receiver harder. She held up her other hand for Sara to wait as her eyes widened.

After what seemed like forever, Keesha got off the phone. Her slender fingers trembled like butterflies' wings as she signed to Sara.

*Amy's mother said that Amy wasn't home.*

*She said if I saw her to tell her that her favorite sweaters are all folded in the drawer waiting for her.* Keesha stopped signing for a moment, took a deep breath and shook her head. *Amy's mother didn't sound right at all. She sounded confused, as if she didn't know what she was saying.*

From that moment, Sara's dismal feeling deepened. In history class, it was all Suzanne Andrews could do to keep Sara's eyes away from Amy's empty chair. But the interpreter didn't succeed in making her pay attention in class.

After the end of the last period, Sara walked into the hall and was shocked to see her brother standing there, talking to George Morrow, the head of Radley Academy. Steve's sand-colored hair hung over his forehead, and there was a grayish cast to his skin. She had seen him only yesterday, but he looked thinner, and worn. There were dark circles under his blue eyes.

Sara hurried to him just as Mr. Morrow turned to walk away. Her fingers flew and her words tumbled over each other. *"Steve! What are you doing here? What's wrong? Something terrible has happened. I can feel it."*

Steve took hold of her hands for a moment. "Slow down. We can't talk here. Let's go outside and get in the car. Then I'll explain."

Sara's hands shook as she put her books in her locker and threw on her coat. She followed her brother outside, where he led her to an unmarked police car.

*"What happened?"* Sara asked as soon as they were sitting inside. She looked deep into her brother's eyes, as if she could find the answer there. Her heart thudded in her chest.

Steve put his hand on Sara's shoulder. He swallowed, and then rubbed a hand over his face.

*"What is it?"* Sara's hands sliced through the air as she spoke.

Too tired and emotionally drained to attempt the signing that he did clumsily at best, Steve said, "What I have to tell you isn't easy."

Sara felt her blood turn to ice.

"It's your friend Amy."

Sara spun around, turning her back to

Steve. *No*, she signed to herself in her thoughts. *No, no, no.*

Steve turned her to face him. Sara forced herself to look at him as he told her, "They found Amy's body near the pond in Shadow Point Park. She's dead."

# Chapter 4

I cannot believe that you are gone, Sara thought as she stood under the canopy at Riverside Cemetery and stared at the pink roses on Amy's casket. Not long ago she had stood under the same canopy and gazed at flowers on another casket, the one that belonged to her father.

Memories came rushing back. The day of her father's burial had been bleak and damp. The air had been heavy with mist that draped the headstones.

The grief that had burned in her veins that day mingled with the bitter ache of today's sorrow. The gray sky shed a harsh, frigid light over the rows of mourners dressed in black. Sara's warm coat couldn't keep out the cold that came from inside. She held a rose in her hand tightly, and didn't notice that the thorns pricked her fingers.

She looked at Amy's mother, Dr. Vera Hendersen. The slight woman looked frail and shrunken — as if Amy's death had sucked her own life out of her. The woman standing in the cemetery was a fragile shell.

Next to Dr. Hendersen stood Mark Royce, his face a stony mask. Something twisted like a knife in Sara's heart. How dare you come here and stand beside her mother? she thought. Words screamed inside her head. You killed her! You killed her!

For an instant their eyes met and Sara's thoughts blazed out of her and washed over him in an acid wave. He dropped his eyes to the ground, and then stared off into the distance.

Sara realized she was trembling all over. Stop it, Sara, she told herself. The newspapers said the death was an accident. Investigators believed Amy had gone walking alongside the pond in the evening. She had slipped, hit her head on rocks at the edge of the pond, and was killed instantly.

Steve swore that the story was true. He had been one of the detectives called to the scene.

A shiver went through Sara's body. The story didn't ring true, especially after all that had happened the day Amy died. Why would Amy go to the park when she said she was meeting Mark at the library?

Mourners were tossing flowers on the coffin. Sara realized that it was time to say her last good-bye. She tried to send a final message to her friend. It was nothing she could put into words, but a reaching out from deep within her heart. Then she tossed her own red rose on Amy's coffin. Her eyes blurred with tears.

When the funeral was over, Sara rode with Keesha and Liz in one of the black limousines that snaked in a long row up Buckeye Ridge. They would all join a gathering of family and friends at the Hendersens' house. The girls sat very still and stared stiffly out of the windows.

Usually Sara was dazzled by the breathtaking view of the Buckeye River from the ridge. Today it didn't move her. She felt hollow inside.

A maid in a crisply starched uniform opened the door to Amy's white-columned house and led the way into a room full of flowers. Several people were already there, and more kept arriving all the time. White lilies stood on the mantle, beside a picture of Amy's smiling face.

Amy's mother, Dr. Hendersen, greeted the girls. She took Sara's hands and held them in her own. "Thank you for coming, Sara. Your friendship meant a lot to Amy."

Sara fought to keep her voice steady as she replied, "It meant a lot to me, too." Her own grief over the death of her father was fresh enough so that she could imagine the pain Amy's mother must be feeling.

"I want to give you something," Dr. Hendersen said before disappearing into another room for a moment. She came back with a slim notebook and placed it in Sara's hands. It was the notebook Amy had used for the history project. Sara recognized the doodles Amy had made all over the cover, and she fought to keep back the tears.

"I think Amy would have wanted you to have it as something to remember her by."

Dr. Hendersen swallowed. For the briefest instant, her lips trembled. "You may find the notes useful." She attempted a smile.

Before Sara realized what was happening, Dr. Hendersen placed something else in her hands. "I also want you to have this sweater. It was a favorite of Amy's, and I know you admired it." She pressed her lips together tightly. "Amy loved sweaters. She had so many."

Sara drew her breath in sharply as she looked at the bright colors. She remembered seeing Amy in that sweater. She couldn't imagine wearing it. She didn't want it. She wanted to push it away.

"Thank you," she said numbly. Sara put the sweater and the notebook on a chair beside her.

"You're welcome." Dr. Hendersen touched Sara's shoulder before she turned and walked away.

Sara had an uneasy tingle at the back of her neck. Someone was watching. She looked around the room and froze as she found her gaze locked with Mark Royce's. He was staring at her, and now he began moving toward her.

A wave of repulsion went through her. I don't want to talk to you, she said to herself. I don't want to be anywhere near you.

She fought an impulse to run from the room. As calmly as she could, she began threading her way through the crowd. She kept walking until she found herself in an empty hallway off the living room. There she stared at the ornate runner on the polished floor while she took deep breaths and tried to calm her racing heart.

She didn't like what she had seen in Mark's eyes just now. They were like two glass marbles resting on the surface of his face, hard and cold, without emotion.

I don't care what the newspapers say, or what my brother tells me, Sara thought. I'm not ready to believe Amy's death was an accident. Maybe I never will believe it.

She leaned against the wall and remembered how Steve had assured her again and again that there was no foul play. But the investigation had been wrapped up much too quickly. Sara's gut feeling was that it was being continued. It had been kept out of the papers, and Steve was keeping it from her.

A tight, searing pain in her wrist cut into her thoughts. She saw Mark's hand on her arm, his fingers gripping it tightly. Sara whirled and looked up into his face.

Mark's face was flushed with anger. "Why do you look at me the way you do, like I'm a criminal? I loved Amy!"

His face was so close that Sara could feel his hot breath. Sara twisted her wrist. "Let go!"

Instead Mark pulled her into an alcove. "Never mind. I just want to ask you for —" But Mark never finished his sentence.

Wayne Hansen prodded his shoulder. "Let go of her!"

Mark dropped Sara's wrist and pushed Wayne aside. He'd begun walking toward the door when Wayne pivoted and thudded his hand into Mark's back.

Suddenly, Mark turned around to face Wayne. The two boys stood there, coiled and ready to pounce. All around them stood the stunned friends and relatives who had come to pay their last respects to Amy.

"Please," Dr. Hendersen stepped between the two boys who towered over her, and made the word a command.

An instant transformation took place in the two boys. Their charged, ready-to-fight posture left them. "I'm so sorry," Mark stammered.

"I didn't mean to hurt you, Sara," Mark said as Wayne apologized to Dr. Hendersen. Then he turned to Amy's mother. "I suppose we should both leave."

"You don't have to leave, Mark," Sara read Dr. Hendersen's lips. "You both will have to control yourselves, however."

Wayne and Mark went to opposite sides of the room. Moments later, Steve arrived to take Sara home.

As soon as he walked in the door Sara was struck by his appearance. His handsome face was clouded with fatigue. He had that ragged look that settles on people when they haven't slept well in days.

When Mark saw Steve, the two of them looked at each other, and Sara saw an unmistakable spark of recognition pass between them. Mark looked from Steve to Sara, a look of surprise passing over his face. Sara understood what had happened. Steve and Mark had met before, and she was willing to bet it was when Steve questioned Mark after Amy's death. Mark had had no idea that Steve was her brother. Now he knew.

## Chapter 5

"*H*ow do you know Mark?" Sara asked the moment they got in the car. "*You questioned him, didn't you? After Amy died?*" she asked before he could answer, her fingers flying.

"Yes," Steve signed back clumsily as he spoke. "*He was Amy's boyfriend.*"

"*I know that. Why didn't you tell me you questioned him?*"

*Police business. Don't have to tell you.* Steve signed.

Sara began signing without speaking, as she sometimes did when she was angry with Steve. *Amy's death was murder. No accident. You're lying and I'm very angry with you.* She scrunched her fingers in front of her face.

*Angry.* When Steve didn't answer, Sara signed, *You're treating me like a child.*

*"You're acting like one, refusing to speak when you know I have trouble with ASL,"* Steve shot back. He fumbled with every word. Sara had to read his lips to make sense of what he was saying.

Though she knew fatigue was partly to blame, Steve's clumsiness with ASL made her even angrier than she already was. She gave him a look that said so.

Sara began speaking again as she signed. *"Amy's body was found in the park. I dropped her off at the library to meet Mark. He must have taken her there."*

Steve raked his hand through his hair and drew in a long breath, as if trying to draw in energy. "I'm too tired to sign any more. I'm sorry. Amy went to the park when Mark didn't show up. She often went there by herself to think."

Steve stopped speaking abruptly. *He's holding something back, I know it.* Sara's insides lurched as if she was on a roller coaster.

Sara punched the air with her hands, giving an angry edge to her signing. *"I know the people Amy knows. I could help you find out who killed her."*

The color drained from Steve's face. Sara knew instantly that she'd made a terrible mistake. From the day she had moved in with him he'd made her understand that he didn't want her to have anything to do with police work.

She jutted her chin out defiantly. She didn't care if Steve was angry. The truth was that every time she got involved in a case she ended up helping to solve it. She tapped her chest. *"I'm a good detective."*

Steve gritted his teeth. He gripped her chin tightly and put his face close to hers. She read his lips. "Don't tell me you're a good detective. Playing at being one has put you in danger before. It's not going to happen again."

Sara twisted out of his grip. "Then you admit that Amy's murderer is out there somewhere?"

Steve grabbed her chin again. "No! But I don't want you snooping around and stirring up trouble. Her mother needs to heal."

Sara turned her head and pushed Steve's hand away. Steve started the car, and they rode back to Thurston Court in silence. As soon as Steve had pulled into a space in the apartment's underground garage, Sara jumped out of the car. She turned to Steve and signed, *B-VOICE,* her name sign for Bret, and ran to her green sedan. If she couldn't talk to Steve about Amy's murder, she hoped she could talk to Bret.

Sara drove north toward Radley University. Bret's parents were on the faculty and lived at the edge of the campus.

The daylight had faded to a smoky twilight. Streetlights had come on in the neighborhood. As Sara drove past downtown Radley, neon signs glowed here and there, and bulbs shimmered in shop windows.

It made her feel better just to think about seeing Bret. Her heart leapt a little every time she saw his broad shoulders and his warm brown eyes. Meeting Bret was one of the best things that had happened to her since she came back to Radley.

Before the basketball season started, Bret

Sanderson had worked part-time at the Radley Free Library. When Sara had asked him for help, he had introduced himself in ASL and explained that although his hearing was normal, his parents were deaf. They joked that they were the only people who could talk in the library without getting in trouble.

Bret and Sara started dating shortly after Sara moved to Radley. Through the past few months their romance had deepened.

Bret was outside when Sara drove up, walking along the sidewalk with his gym bag slung over his shoulder. He wore a short, heavy black jacket that zipped up the front and a pair of faded jeans. Sara loved the way he walked, with an easy, swinging gait that made him look as if he had just heard a piece of good news and was eager to go and share it with someone. He waved to her as she drove up.

*Hello,* he signed to Sara as she got out of the car. *I just got back from basketball practice.*

Bret's arms circled Sara. He pulled her to

him and kissed her lightly on the mouth. Then he kissed her again, more tenderly and deeper than before.

Sara breathed deeply. Her heart beat faster as she leaned against him. It was so good to feel his arms around her.

They held each other. When they parted Sara signed, *Amy's funeral was today.*

Bret nodded. He brushed a strand of Sara's brown hair off her forehead gently. He had never met Amy, but Sara had told him about her. He took Sara's hand and led her into the house.

The Sandersons' home was snug and low-ceilinged, with an accent on comfort. The couches and chairs showed signs of plenty of use. The place was chock-full of books, in floor-to-ceiling shelves on the living room walls, in bookcases in the study and the bedrooms — even in the kitchen.

Bret led Sara to the kitchen table. He opened a wooden cabinet and took out two cups and set them on the counter. *Tea?*

Sara shook her head and signed back, *No. Thanks.*

Bret took a deep, square pan from the

counter and removed the checkered cloth that covered it. He signed, *Brownies.*

Usually, Sara loved Mrs. Sanderson's brownies. They were dark, rich, and dense, thick with walnuts and chocolate chips. Every bite flooded your mouth with a rich chocolately taste.

Today, they didn't tempt her. I might as well be looking at a tin of plaster, she thought as she looked at them. Her mouth felt pasty.

Bret put the pan back on the counter. He hit his forehead with the heel of his hand. Then he circled his heart. *Stupid. Sorry.* He touched the side of her face gently, then signed. *You're too upset to eat.*

Sara nodded. Her fingers flew as she told Bret everything that had happened. It was a relief to talk to somebody who didn't have any trouble understanding ASL. She was eager to know his thoughts.

Sara finished her story and looked at Bret expectantly. She was surprised to see his features darken with anger.

*What's the matter?* she signed.

Bret glared at her. *Don't you pay any attention to what I say? I've told you that I don't like you poking your nose into police investigations. It's dangerous.*

Sara was stunned. She felt as if she'd been plunged into a deep freeze without warning.

Bret scowled at her. *Why do you look so surprised? I guess it's true. You don't pay attention to what I say.* He stood up from the table abruptly. His six-foot-tall form towered over Sara. *Grow up, Sara. Leave the police work to the police. Don't play detective.*

Sara stood up so fast she knocked her chair to the floor. *You're acting just like my brother. I thought you would understand.* She didn't stop to pick up the chair. She grabbed her coat from the closet and put it on as she raced out of Bret's house.

Sara didn't look back as she ran down the walk to her car. As she slid behind the wheel she didn't glance up to see if Bret was standing in the doorway. She drove away from his house, feeling as if a brick wall had suddenly been thrown up between them. She thought they had grown so close, but now they seemed so far apart.

Drops of rain began to dot the windshield as Sara drove toward downtown Radley. By the time she had passed the business district and was nearing Thurston Court, the rain had settled into a steady patter.

Sara bit her lip. Amy was dead, Steve wouldn't tell her the truth, and now she and Bret were fighting.

As she drove, Sara realized that this was one of the few times she hoped Steve wasn't home when she got there. She prayed he had gone back to work — or out to see his girl-friend, Marisa Douglas. She hated being in the apartment alone, but she didn't want to see Steve now.

A sudden jolt nearly knocked Sara out of her seat. It was followed by another and another.

Someone was deliberately ramming into her car. Sara gripped the steering wheel tightly and glanced at the rearview mirror. What she saw made her breath catch in her throat.

Inside the car behind her, pairs of vicious, burning eyes seemed to float in space. The car rammed into her again.

They're all wearing ski masks, she realized after a moment. She pressed her foot on the accelerator. In the mirror she saw the license plate numbers blur as the car sped up. Then she caught a glimpse of a word: retro.

The car pulled alongside hers. Sara saw the driver turn the wheel sharply to the right. Fear closed in as she realized they were trying to force her off the road.

# Chapter 6

Steel scraped against steel as the dark car slammed into Sara's door. Sara skidded and felt her right wheels thud off into the gravel on the shoulder of the road.

The dark car pulled away and prepared for another jolt. Sara jerked her steering wheel to the left and pulled back onto the roadway.

Within seconds the dark car piled into her again, this time nearly succeeding in forcing her completely off the road. Once more, Sara jerked the steering wheel to the left and got the car out of the gravel.

*Think! Think!* she signed to herself in her thoughts. She jammed her foot down on the accelerator and shot ahead of the other car.

There's so much more road without an intersection, she thought fearfully.

It only took a few moments for the car to overtake her. She slowed down, and so did they. They teased her by edging closer, closer, then pulling away.

Sara sped up again. When the dark car pulled alongside her, she sped up some more. Then she pulled her foot off the accelerator as quickly as she dared, rapidly slowing to a crawl.

The move bought her a little time, but not much. The other car slowed down and was soon beside her. She could tell that the faces behind the ski masks were laughing. They were enjoying themselves. A bolt of anger shot through her.

They were approaching an intersection. Sara sped up again, inching the speedometer higher than she ever dared before. She hoped to beat them to the intersection and turn off toward more well-traveled roads.

The dark car surged ahead. Clearly it was a faster car than her own green sedan. As they approached the intersection, the dark car pulled in front of her and then slowed to a stop. Sara slammed on the brakes to avoid a collision.

The door on the driver's side of the car ahead opened. Sara's palms felt cold as she realized the driver was getting out. Then the other doors opened and the other boys got out too. Sara's heart lodged in her throat.

The driver was a tall boy with a strange, heavy-footed walk. He was obviously the leader. No one moved until he did; then they all followed.

Sara didn't have to know body language to see the threat in the tall boy's walk. Behind him the other boys fell in line, creeping slowly behind him. Sara could feel them all enjoying her fear.

Suddenly, they were all drenched in a blaze of headlights. Two other cars had just turned onto the road.

As other drivers slowed down to see what was going on, the driver of the dark car ran and jumped back behind the wheel. The other boys quickly followed him and got into the car. The dark car sped away and disappeared into the night.

\* \* \*

*If those cars hadn't shown up when they did, who knows what could have happened?* Sara signed to Keesha as they walked to school the next morning. Everything looks so different in the daylight, she thought as she looked at the neat rows of townhouses that shimmered in the chilly morning sun. Last night her frightening ordeal had bathed all the streets in an ominous glow, and all of the buildings that loomed out of the darkness had a threatening quality.

In the underground parking lot at Thurston Court, Sara kept seeing things in the shadows. In the elevator her heart pounded all the way to the seventh floor.

When she found the apartment empty, she had gone immediately to Keesha's door. Mrs. Fletcher's mouth had dropped open when she saw Sara's pale, trembling form and her wide, frightened eyes.

It had helped to pour out her story to Keesha — all about the terrifying car chase, and her fights with Steve and Bret. The two girls were so in tune with each other, Sara felt soothed by her friend's understanding. She confided that she suspected Steve was working on an undercover investigation of Amy's death.

As the girls entered the school building Keesha turned to Sara and asked, "Did you tell Steve what happened with the car last night?"

Sara shook her head and signed, *No. He was at the police station. Later.*

She wanted — needed — to get over last night's battle. She hoped that when she went to report the crime, they would be able to clear the air.

Moments later, as the girls stood by her locker, Sara saw Keesha giving her an appraising once-over. *You don't look well, Sara. Are you sick?*

Sara shrugged, though she was afraid the answer was yes. Ever since she had awakened that morning she had been trying to deny the raw, dry feeling in her throat, the burning sensation behind her eyes. On top of everything else, it felt as if she had a bad cold coming on. She began rifling through her locker when she felt a tug on her arm. Keesha pointed to the end of the hall.

A group of students were gathered under the clock near the main bulletin board and the trophy case. They formed an expanding crowd.

The girls slammed their lockers shut and hurried to see what was going on. As they approached, they could see that two students — Joel Winters and Karen Lee — were the focus of all the commotion.

Sara could see the outline of Joel's portable electronic organizer in the pocket of his white button-down shirt. Behind the thick panes of his glasses, his eyes were beaming. His face had temporarily lost its perpetually startled expression. His thin arms and legs were moving with excitement.

Beside Joel stood Karen, more reserved than Joel but radiating the pride she felt inside. There was a quiet elegance about her, a simplicity in the way she dressed and wore her hair pulled back casually and held with a clasp at the nape of her neck. Though Karen was of average height, about as tall as Sara, she still had a few inches on Joel.

Keesha asked questions and signed to Sara. *They posted the names of the students from Radley Academy who qualified to take the exam for the Radley Business Association College Scholarship. Joel and Karen both made it.*

Sara looked at the list. A third student from Radley had qualified. Mark Royce.

She caught a glimpse of Mark out of the corner of her eye. He wasn't smiling like the other two. His face was blank, his eyes staring far away. Sara wondered what was going through his mind. A tiny chill ran along her spine.

Mark caught Sara looking at him. He walked over and stood squarely in front of her. "I guess I don't expect you to congratulate me." Sara turned to walk away, and he put a hand on her arm. "Wait. Please. Look, I hope that in time you'll believe that I didn't hurt Amy. I loved her."

Mark's clothing was wrinkled and there were dark circles under his eyes. His broad shoulders sagged, and his face had an ashen hue. He took a deep breath and raked a hand through his hair. "What I want to say is —

after the funeral yesterday I saw Amy's mother give you a notebook of hers. I know Amy doodled my name, and 'Mark & Amy' all over it. It would mean a lot to me to have it. That's what I was trying to ask you for yesterday. I'm sorry."

"You can have the notebook, but not right now."

Mark scowled. "Why can't I have it now?"

"Amy and I were working on a project together. I need to look at her notes."

The scowl deepened. Sara saw Mark's jaw tighten.

"Look — Amy tucked a couple photos in the back flap. I'd like to have them. Just give them to me."

"The notebook is at home," Sara lied. "I'll look tonight — give you the photos tomorrow."

Mark stood there staring at her, his eyes glowering. His face was clouded with resentment.

Sara shot Mark a warning look. She wasn't about to let him make her his new target. After a beat he whirled and stalked down the hall.

When she turned around, Sara nearly bumped into Joel Winters. "Royce sure is a grouch," he said. It was obvious that he had heard the whole conversation. Sara recalled that Joel liked to eavesdrop, enjoyed over-hearing gossip.

Joel didn't seem to care about gossip right now, though. He was grinning broadly. He pointed to his name on the list. "See that? See my name?" he asked. Without waiting for an answer, he turned and walked away. He was chuckling to himself.

As the day went on, Mark kept popping up wherever Sara turned. In the cafeteria and in the halls she would see him staring at her, a grudging, sullen expression on his face. Sara couldn't wait until the school day ended, so that she could be away from him — and so that she could see Steve.

The moment her last class ended, Sara hurried to the parking lot, her eyes darting right and left, on the lookout for Mark Royce. She managed to avoid him.

As she drove toward the precinct, her pulse quickened with a mixture of anxiety and anticipation. She wanted to find out if there had been any incidents involving dangerous joyriders in a dark car. When she made her report she would have an opportunity to set things straight between her and Steve.

Soon the small city building that served as Radley's Fourth Precinct police station was in sight. Sara steered the sedan to the corner of Penn and Harrison and pulled into a parking space. As she got out of the car and headed inside, she inhaled the familiar chocolate and vanilla aroma from the Buckeye Foods Bakery down the street. Normally she enjoyed it, but today her stomach was tight with tension; the heavy odor sent it into flips.

Inside the station Sara nodded to the desk officer and swept past the bulletin board full of wanted posters and announcements. She took the stairs to Steve's office two at a time. At the end of the narrow hallway was the office he shared with other detectives on rotating shifts.

She let out a sigh of regret when she saw that the office was empty. Her brother's desk was covered with files and papers. Beyond it the top drawer to the file cabinet was pulled out to reveal the manila folders inside.

Sara's heart leapt. She had discovered information in Steve's office before. She flashed a glance over her shoulder. She couldn't risk being caught.

Sara crept to the doorway, and peered into the hall. No one was there. She sat down in the swivel chair at Steve's desk and stared at the pile in front of her. She'd have to be careful to cover her tracks so that Steve wouldn't suspect she'd been snooping.

Sara was reaching for a folder when, out of the corner of her eye, she saw Lt. Rosemary Marino entering the office. Her heart sank.

The Community Liaison Officer had worked with Sara's father. She always attempted to sign some words to Sara, though her vocabulary of ASL was limited. Now she pushed her fingers forward and flipped her pinky, signing *Hi*.

Sara returned the greeting and then read Lt. Marino's lips. "I'm not sure when Steve will be back. Is there anything I can do for you?"

As a matter of fact, you can, Sara thought.

She remembered the lieutenant's hobby was collecting the names people used on their vanity plates. She copied them down when the plates came over the printouts of stolen car reports or the tow sheets from the RPD lot. She posted them on the bulletin board over her desk.

"Have you ever heard of a license plate, RETRO?

Lt. Marino's eyes crinkled as she tried to understand Sara's muffled speech.

"License plate," Sara repeated. She grabbed a pen and a scrap of paper from Steve's desk and scribbled, R E T R O.

Her brow furrowed as Lt. Marino repeated, "retro." She frowned. "I don't think so. Come with me." Sara followed the lieutenant to her office, where they both scanned the list posted on her bulletin board. "I don't recall that plate," said Lt. Marino. "We can check the computer. Want to tell me what this is about?"

"Check first," Sara urged. "Please."

They were still at the computer when Steve entered the office. His eyes widened with surprise when he saw Sara. "What's going on?"

"Sara had a little run-in with another car last night," Marino explained. "She saw the letters R-E-T-R-O on the license plate. But I can't find any RETRO in the computer." Lt. Marino's mouth dropped open. A chuckle escaped her lips. She put her hand over her mouth and looked as if she was enjoying a private joke — with herself.

"Sara," she said after a moment. "When you saw this RETRO, it was in the rearview mirror, wasn't it?"

Sara understood at once. She slapped her forehead with her hand. *Stupid.* Of course. She had been looking at the letters backwards.

Lt. Marino was still chuckling. "I think what you saw was ORTER. Part of TRANSPORTER. The car had transporter plates. Those are the plates used car lots use."

Steve spoke up. "There are loads of used car lots around Radley. If we don't have anything else to go on, that car will be impossible to trace." He turned to Sara. "You still haven't told me what's going on."

Haltingly, speaking and signing, Sara filled Steve in on what happened the night before.

As her story went on, she could see him get more and more alarmed.

*No driving.* He signed when she finished. *Too dangerous until we catch these kids.*

Sara was stunned. *"No,"* she blurted out as she signed. *"Not fair. I'll be careful."*

Steve shook his head. "I'm your guardian and I have to keep you safe."

Anger flamed through Sara. There he goes again, treating me like a child, when he is hardly any older than I am. "No!" she snapped. "You can't take away my car!" She ran from the station, tears of rage stinging her eyes.

Sara brushed the tears from her face with the back of her hand as she got into her car. She had come to the police station with the hope of making things right between them. Now it was worse than ever.

She drove around aimlessly for over an hour. The last thing she wanted to do was go home to the empty apartment.

Then she passed the library, and decided to go in. The warm, wood-paneled rooms and the bustle of activity usually gave her a feeling of comfort. Perhaps she could lose herself in a book for a while. She pulled the car into a parking space and started up the walk.

The area in front of the library was darker than usual, she noticed. Then she understood why. One of the glass lanterns that stood on either side of the building had been broken. From the looks of things, it had only happened recently. Broken glass still lay on the sidewalk. Someone probably threw a rock, she thought.

Sara shivered in the night air. She drew her collar up around her neck and clutched the strap of her book bag. A chill crept into her bones. As she approached the steps an image of Amy flashed into her mind. The last time Sara had seen her, Amy had been running up these steps.

A wary, tingling feeling surged through Sara's body tightening the skin at the back of her neck. Her eyes searched the darkness.

There was a single moment when Sara knew with terrible certainty that something was about to happen. In that same instant a shadowy figure shot from the bushes and hurled toward her.

Panic pumped through her veins and exploded in her brain. She saw the glint of something shiny as the light from the moon flashed along its edge.

*Chapter 7*

In the moonlight, the blade glistened as the knife arced through the air. Sara closed her eyes and turned her face away. She waited for the pain.

It never came. Sara opened her eyes. Stunned, she watched her attacker run into the bushes, his gait lurching and clumsy. She looked around and saw a piece of her book bag strap, the edge raw and ragged. The attacker had cut the book bag off her arm.

Sara's heart was racing. She breathed in great gulps of air, relieved. Then heavy pulses of anger began to throb steadily in her heart.

She was just beginning to catch her breath, when suddenly a stoop-shouldered, elderly man trotted up to her, his face puckered with alarm. Tufts of white hair stood out all over his head like wisps of white cotton candy. He began gesturing wildly, and talking very fast. Sara leaned toward him and stared, straining to pick up what he was saying.

When she didn't reply, the little man became even more agitated. He shook his head from side to side, his mouth moving all the time.

Sara looked at his frightened face and waving arms and felt his excitement adding to her own. Then Sara's natural, steady control took hold. She began to understand what was the matter with the man. *He must have heard me scream, or seen the struggle. He wants to help.*

Sara held her hands out, palms up, gesturing for him to slow down. She touched her ear and shook her head. She signed *Deaf* as she said the word aloud.

After a moment, comprehension spread over the man's features. He smiled at her, with a faint trace of apology, and tapped her gently on the shoulder.

Sara felt herself trembling as she watched the man disappear into the bushes. Now that the danger was over, she felt shaken and weak.

In a minute the man returned, carrying her book bag, and the dirt-streaked books and papers that had been scattered on the ground. He handed them to her, and tilted his head in a slight bow. Then he was gone.

Sara looked through the pile in her hands. There was nothing missing. She decided that her attacker was looking for money. He must have assumed her wallet was in her bag.

Then she noticed that something was missing after all. It was the notebook Amy's mother had given her — the one with the notes for the history project.

"Don't you think you should tell your brother what happened?" Walking backwards, Keesha spoke to Sara as the two girls walked to school the next morning. She'd had lots of practice walking backwards; that way Sara would read her lips and watch her hands when she signed.

Sara's breath came out in white clouds. "No way."

She explained how Steve acted when she

told him about her run-in with the joyriders. Keesha's eyes widened as Sara told her how Steve had tried to make her stop driving until they were caught, even though he didn't have any leads. *"I felt like he wanted to punish me."* Sara struck her bent elbow with her index finger. *Punish.*

"He wasn't punishing you," Keesha said.

Sara let her breath out in a white puff. "I know. But that's how it felt." She remembered how Steve had kept her from doing things before, or had her secretly followed by an officer. Her chest tightened at the memory.

The girls' feet crunched over the frozen ground. "I couldn't tell Steve much about the guy anyway," Sara said. "Except that he was big."

Keesha stopped walking as they reached the door to the school. "Was he as big as Mark?"

Sara nodded.

"Do you think it was Mark?"

Sara signed back, *Don't know.*

The girls entered the school and joined the throng of students that surged through the halls.

Sara opened her locker and jumped when an envelope fell out and nearly hit her on the head. She gasped as photographs scattered over the tile floor. They were from Liz Martinson's party. Amy's smiling face looked out from some of the glossy surfaces.

Sara had gathered up the pictures on the day of the big scene in the cafeteria. They had almost been left behind. Now she bent down and shoved them back into the envelope.

As she stood up she found Mark Royce standing in front of her. He glanced at the envelope in her hand. Sara wondered if he'd seen the pictures of Amy lying on the floor.

"Are you finished with Amy's history notebook?" he asked without bothering to say hello. "I'd really like to have it." He looked down at Sara, his expression showing clearly that he expected her to hand it over immediately.

"I don't have it anymore. It was stolen last night." Sara watched him carefully, trying to gauge his reaction.

For a moment he looked at her blankly. Then his lip curled into a sneer. "Oh, come on."

"It's true," Sara insisted.

Mark's face clouded with resentment. He banged his fist on a locker before he turned and stalked away.

Keesha looked at Sara and signed, *I think you ought to stay away from him.*

Sara thought Keesha had a point. She just couldn't think of a way to investigate Amy's murder without getting near Mark Royce.

"I didn't get a chance to congratulate you on qualifying for the Business Association Scholarship Exam the other day," Sara remarked as she passed by Joel Winters in biology. Then she caught her breath. Joel was one of the students in the class working on an individual project. She only realized at that moment that it involved dissecting a frog.

Sara was about to turn her face away when Joel looked up at her, with the same childish grin of delight as the day before.

"Thank you," he said. His eyes were shining. Then he went back to dissecting the frog with a small, sharp-pointed knife. Sara noticed that the smile didn't leave his face.

Suzanne Andrews tapped her arm and motioned her into her seat. Sara noticed that everyone else was sitting down and class was about to start. *You're so distracted today, Sara,* Ms. Andrews signed.

*I know,* Sara signed. *Sorry.*

Sara took her seat and turned her attention to Suzanne as she signed the teacher's words. *Everyone who's not involved in an individual project please take out your lab manuals.*

Sara discovered that she had forgotten hers. She looked at Ms. Andrews apologetically. *I'm going to have to go and get the book from my locker,* she signed.

A line creased the interpreter's forehead. She stared after Sara as she left the room, a look of concern on her face.

Moments later Sara was heading down the empty hall toward her locker. *It's no wonder I'm distracted,* she said to herself.

The wound caused by her father's death was still healing, but the pain had begun to dull. Sara was just beginning to feel comfortable in the hearing world when her life had been turned upside down all over again. A close friend had been killed. Sara had been mugged. Her relationships with her brother and her boyfriend were strained.

I'm entitled to be a little distracted, Sara said to herself.

As she approached her locker she stopped suddenly. The door was open, and a man was standing there. He was going through her locker!

"Hey!" Sara called out.

The man turned around. When Sara realized who it was, a dull flush of embarrassment began to spread up from her collar. It was only one of the janitors, Charlie Dolan — the one everybody called "Dandy" because he was always smoothing and combing his hair. He was often spotted checking his reflection in the glass of the trophy case.

Now Dandy Dolan took out his comb and stroked it idly through his hair as he pulled back his lips and sent a smile pouring across his face.

"Hey, yourself, Sara Howell," he said. Dandy's shirtsleeves were rolled up and Sara noticed for the first time that a dark tattoo of a snake slithered up his forearm.

She frowned. "What's going on?"

"Maybe something, maybe nothing," the janitor said in a drawl that wasn't easy for Sara to read. The grin on Dolan's face grew broader, as if he had an amusing secret. "Did you remember you left your locker door open and come back to close it?"

Sara's eye flickered over the man's face. She noticed that his wide smile wasn't reflected in his eyes.

"No."

The smile disappeared. "Well, maybe you forgot. Then again, maybe you didn't, and someone broke into your locker. Come over here and see if anything is missing."

Sara stepped over to her locker and looked inside. Books were stacked neatly on the shelves. Her coat was hanging up.

"I don't think anything is missing."

Charlie Dolan smiled again. "Well, then let's just make sure the lock is working." He closed the door. "Try it."

Sara waited until Charlie moved back before she spun the combination. The lock clicked, she pulled the handle. The door opened smoothly. "It's okay."

Again, the broad smile. "That's good. I'll be going, then. Make sure you always keep that door closed."

"Right."

Sara watched the janitor walk away. There was something about him she didn't like. The signals that he gave her didn't match up — like the way he kept smiling, but the smile never reached his eyes.

She turned back to her locker and got out the book for class. There's no harm done, she told herself. After all, nothing was stolen.

Then Sara reminded herself of how distracted she had been lately. Maybe I did leave the locker open, she thought.

It was with mixed feelings that she decided to report the incident. She stopped into the office after lunch.

"May I help you?" Ms. Finster asked from behind the counter, clicking her ballpoint pen with one hand while her other hand patted the scarf at her neck. Sara noticed that Ms. Finster was alone in the office. It seemed to be making her nervous.

Ms. Finster was a new administrative assistant who had been assigned the responsibility of investigating locker break-ins. She was about thirty, with pale gray eyes and a sweet, anxious expression. She reminded Sara of someone who is lost and in a hurry, but is afraid to ask directions.

As usual, Ms. Finster's glasses were perched atop her brown hair like a tiara. She pulled them onto her face and peered at Sara through the lenses.

"Yes, well . . ." Suddenly Sara felt foolish. Ms. Finster continued to peer at her, looking so curious Sara imagined a cartoon question mark floating in the air above her head.

Joel Winters pushed open the door and came up to stand close behind Sara. She had a feeling he was trying to listen to what she and Ms. Finster were saying, but ignored him and forged ahead.

"I found Charlie Dolan going through my locker between classes. He said he'd found the door open and was just checking it."

At the mention of Charlie Dolan's name, Ms. Finster's eyebrows shot up. "Goodness! Was anything stolen?"

"No," Sara said, gazing in wonder at the alarm on Ms. Finster's face. "It was just — odd."

Ms. Finster cocked her head and pursed her lips. "I always thought that Charlie Dolan was an odd one, all right." She leaned across the counter. She looked as if she was about to share a secret with Sara. "I think there is something shady about him."

Sara couldn't help smiling as she realized Ms. Finster was whispering. I should remind her not to bother, she thought.

Suddenly the smile disappeared from Sara's face. Ms. Finster had gone pale. Her mouth opened, but Sara couldn't understand what she was saying.

Then she realized that Ms. Finster was screaming.

*Chapter 8*

A stack of books and papers that had been piled on a table in the corner went flying into the air. Sara turned and saw the cause of all the commotion. It was the man she and Ms. Finster had just been talking about — Charlie Dolan.

The janitor wasn't the smooth, oily character he had been earlier, when Sara caught him going through her locker. This was Charlie Dolan on a rampage. He reminded Sara of Mark Royce in one of his fits of temper.

With a snarl at Joel and Sara, Charlie stomped behind the counter and went straight for Ms. Finster. Sara couldn't move. It was as if her legs had grown roots.

"What's going on?" she asked a pale and trembling Joel Winters.

He didn't answer. Instead, he ran from the room. Joel is certainly no hero, Sara thought fleetingly.

Ms. Finster fumbled in a desk drawer and brought out an envelope. She handed it to Charlie Dolan.

The envelope had a magical effect. Dolan calmed down immediately. Apparently he had gotten what he came for and didn't want to cause any more trouble. Clutching it firmly in his hand, he strode from the office without a backwards glance.

Sara ran behind the counter. Ms. Finster was leaning weakly against a desk. One hand was pressed to her heart. Sara helped her into a chair, where she sat with her eyes closed and her hand still against her chest.

Poor Ms. Finster, thought Sara as she fetched her a cup of water. She was so easily frightened that she had probably been tormented all through school, with rubber insects and other practical jokes, anything to scare the daylights out of her. Now something truly frightening had happened. It must be a nightmare for her.

Ms. Finster took a few sips of water, and then began fanning herself. After a few more minutes she was able to tell Sara what had happened.

Charlie Dolan had stormed into the office threatening to wreck the place if he didn't get his paycheck immediately. He knew enough to pick a time when the rest of the staff was at lunch and Ms. Finster would be alone.

Dolan wasn't supposed to get his check until the following day, but he said he needed it because he was leaving town immediately. Of course, he hadn't said why he was leaving.

"I knew I was right about him," Ms. Finster said. "There is something wrong with that man."

Why was Charlie Dolan in such a hurry to leave town? Sara asked herself for what seemed like the millionth time that evening. She sat in the den, trying to do her homework. She wasn't having much success. Her thoughts kept jumping from one thing to another — Amy's death, problems with Bret and Steve, and Charlie Dolan.

The lights blinked on and off. Sara turned and saw Steve in the doorway, his hand on the light switch.

*Hi,* he signed.

Sara signed back. *Hi.* She welcomed the sight of her brother, hoping that they could finally settle things. There were dark circles under Steve's eyes. *You look tired,* Sara signed.

Steve sank down on the couch and put his briefcase down beside him. His shoulders slumped. "I am tired. Too tired to sign." He shrugged apologetically.

Sara gave a dismissive wave with her hand.

Steve ran a hand over his face, as if trying to wipe away the fatigue. "I'm sorry we quarreled yesterday. You were right. I shouldn't have told you not to drive. It's just that I worry about you and want you to be safe." Steve spread his hands out helplessly. "Detective. Father. Brother. Too much sometimes."

Sara touched her closed hand to her forehead and flicked her index finger upward. *Understand*. She touched her hand to her brother's cheek, and watched a smile spread over his weary face.

"Want to go out for dinner, Sara? It would give us a chance to do some catching up."

Sara held up both palms and pushed them forward. *Terrific*.

Steve repeated the sign. *Terrific*. He got up from the couch. "I'll just take a quick shower and I'll be ready in no time." He headed in the direction of the bathroom.

When he was gone Sara began gathering up her books and papers. She was taking them to her bedroom when the light over the doorbell flashed.

Sara opened the door and saw Keesha standing there, a worried look on her face. Sara drew her inside.

Keesha began signing rapidly. *Something strange just happened. Someone called me wanting to leave a message for you.*

*Who?* Sara looked at her quizzically.

*Don't know*. Keesha's expression was a

mixture of confusion and panic. *Said you'd better give them the negatives. Then suddenly, the person hung up. It sounded like someone came into the room. I heard yelling in the background.* Keesha's hand suddenly stopped moving.

Steve had come into the room. He was wearing a T-shirt and beige slacks, and was towel-drying his hair. Although he hadn't finished dressing, he already had his beeper on.

Keesha and Sara exchanged nervous glances. Steve took one look at them and lowered the towel from his head. "What's wrong?" he asked slowly. "You two look awfully tense."

"There is nothing wrong, Steve," Sara said as firmly and convincingly as she could. She held her breath as Steve gave her an appraising look. After a moment he glanced down at the beeper that was clipped to his belt.

Thank goodness, thought Sara. His beeper went off. She watched as he picked up a pencil, jotted down a number, and made a phone call. Sara watched as he held the receiver to his ear, frowning, his lips pressed tightly to-gether.

"I'm sorry, Sara," he said when he finished the call. "I won't be able to have dinner tonight. Something has come up."

Whatever Steve's message had been, it apparently had wiped away his suspicions of moments ago. Sara was so relieved that she didn't mind the cancellation. "That's all right," she said, and meant it.

About half an hour earlier, Charlie Dolan had been headed toward the interstate, his foot pressed firmly on the gas pedal. "Get me out of here," he said to himself. "The sooner I put Radley behind me, the better." He tapped his fingers on the steering wheel.

Through the windshield he kept glancing at the huge, brightly painted initials CD he had painted on the hood. Now he wished he hadn't. They made the car too easy to spot. He promised himself he'd have them painted over — just as soon as he got far enough away from Radley.

Charlie Dolan had always lived alone, and

preferred it that way. Like many people who live alone, he had developed the habit of talking to himself. When he was nervous, as he was now, he did it even more than usual.

He began rambling on and on in a one-way conversation. With a glance at his face in the mirror, he asked himself, "Charlie, why did you ever get mixed up with that crazy kid? You knew he was trouble." Dolan shook his head. "Charlie, you never learn. But you're smart to get out while you can. This situation is getting hotter than a firecracker, and you're right in the middle."

Charlie Dolan licked his lips. "That poor kid, Amy. What a shame. All because of that crazy boy. It wasn't my fault, though. No, no, not my fault."

Inside, a little voice squeaked at him, Yes, it was, Charlie. Yes, it was.

There was a yellow light up ahead. Charlie cursed when he saw it, and floored the gas pedal. He sailed past the light as it turned red. "All right!" Charlie grinned, pleased with himself for a moment. The smile vanished from his face and he became morose once more.

Charlie made a left turn and eased the car onto the downhill road that eventually would take him to the interstate. "Come on, come on, Charlie," he said to himself. "Get out while the getting is good. Bye-bye, Radley. Bye-bye, you twisted, sick kid."

He was fast coming up to another light. "Damn!" he said when he saw it turn red.

Just beyond the stoplight was an overpass. As Charlie slowed to pull up at the light, a boulder came hurtling down from it, aimed to hit Charlie's windshield dead center.

Charlie raised his eyes a fraction of a second before it hit, and knew there was nothing he could do. He also knew this was no freak accident. It had been carefully planned.

The boulder struck the windshield, shattering the safety glass. The impact made Charlie shoot forward in his seat. As usual, he wasn't wearing a seatbelt, but Charlie didn't have time to regret it before his head struck the dashboard.

Charlie bounced backwards as the car spun around and into the path of oncoming traffic. At the last minute, he took his hands from the steering wheel and flung his arms around his head, over his eyes. Then came the crash.

# Chapter 9

Sara sat on the rug in the den, her arms wrapped around her knees and the flickering light from the television casting shadows on her face. Beside her, his head nestled between his paws, was Tuck.

Sara flipped through the channels with the remote, barely pausing to read the closed captions. She hadn't really come in here to watch television. She had come in to be close to her father, as she sometimes did when she was alone.

Paul Howell had used the room as an office, and the room was full of reminders of him. His favorite books still stood in the bookshelves. His smiling face looked out from the pictures on the walls. Sara imagined him sitting at his desk and turning to her, the corners of his eyes crinkled as if he had just thought of something funny.

In the months since his death she had gradually come to feel more comfort here than grief. Now she looked at her father's picture and spoke to him with her heart.

You always told me to trust my instincts, Dad. Now they're telling me that Amy was murdered. How do I find her killer? Where do I look? What do I do? Give me a sign.

Tuck stirred beside her, and nudged her with his nose. What do you want? she asked him silently as she gently ruffled his fur. Tuck was staring at the television screen.

Sara took a look and suddenly was riveted by what she saw. It was some sort of news bulletin, and a reporter was interviewing her brother!

The location was the scene of an accident. Sara recognized the road that led to the outskirts of Radley and merged with the interstate. In the background she saw the ruined remains of a car, its windshield shattered. An ambulance flashed a red glow over the scene.

So this is what the beeper message was about, she thought.

From reading the captions, Sara learned the rest of the story. She hugged her knees tighter as it unfolded.

When the police arrived they found the car in the middle of the road, the driver unconscious and slumped over the steering wheel. The boulder that had shattered the windshield and caused the car to go out of control was embedded in the twisted metal of the hood.

Sara paled and sat up straighter as she learned that there were no boulders on the overpass near where the accident had occurred. Police believed that someone had brought the boulder from the woods nearby, and caused the accident deliberately by pushing it down onto the windshield. Miraculously, no other people were hurt when the driver lost control of the vehicle.

Detectives thought that the crime had all the earmarks of a gang of vandals who'd been responsible for other acts of random violence around Radley recently. However, they hadn't ruled out other possibilities. They were asking for any information relating to the accident. An eight-hundred number flashed on the screen.

The broadcast concluded with the announcement that the driver would be taken to East End General Hospital. Sara gasped when she read his name. Charles Dolan.

She had a sixth sense that the accident wasn't random violence at all. She thought Dolan must be somehow tangled in the web surrounding Amy's murder, but she had no idea how.

That night Sara tossed and turned. The questions in her mind flitted in and out of her dreams like dark, twisted shadows that refused to reveal what they were hiding.

Sara woke to find that the cold that had been threatening her had finally appeared. Her throat was raw and stinging, her head felt clogged and the area behind her eyelids felt hot. She started to heave herself out of bed and get ready for school anyway, when she remembered that it was Saturday. She flung herself back against the pillows.

For the next several hours Sara alternated

between fitful sleep and dazed awakenings. Once she thought she saw Steve, and thought he may have even spoken to her. Later she wondered if it had been only a dream.

The last time she woke up the clock told her it was four in the afternoon. Sara called out for Steve, but he didn't appear.

Steve sometimes worked all night, even on weekends, when he was especially busy with a heavy caseload. Sara knew he might not come home at all. She didn't want to stay in the apartment by herself all night.

Determined to get up, she told herself she wasn't very sick. She rolled out of bed and padded to the bathroom. There she took a steaming hot shower that she hoped would clear her head. It didn't, but she emerged from the bathroom feeling slightly better than before.

The cold wasn't the only reason she felt sick and miserable, she knew. Part of it was the reminder that Saturday nights were usually spent with Bret. But not this one.

She grabbed a quick bite to eat then checked the TTY for messages. None. The only message was the folded note she found on the dining room table. It was from Steve, telling her to take care of her cold (I did see him after all, she thought) and that he was working late. Again.

We're on our own, Tuck, Sara told him with her eyes. She dressed quickly in jeans and a sweater, then snapped on Tuck's leash. *I'm sorry I didn't take you out before,* she signed. She stuffed some tissues into the pocket of her coat. Then they took the elevator to the underground garage.

By the time Sara got out on the road, the sky had just begun to turn the color of winter twilight. Sara considered going to the Side Door Café for a cup of their rich, delicious hot chocolate, but quickly decided against it.

The Side Door was near the university, in the same part of town as Bret's house. There was a fairly good chance that she'd run into Bret there, and he would probably think she had deliberately sought him out. Sara didn't want that, especially since it would be partially true. Besides, with her cold she couldn't taste hot chocolate anyway.

Sara pulled up in front of the library. Where to go? What to do? she asked herself.

Keesha and Liz both had dates, she knew. For a moment, and only a moment, she allowed herself to feel blue and alone.

That's enough, she told herself, giving her shoulders a shake. She would take a walk around the square. The lights in the park had just been turned on, making it look quaint and festive. As she reached for Tuck's leash, something on the floor of the car caught her eye. She picked it up.

It was a book, blue with a silver border and gold-edged pages. There was a little strap on it, with a clasp. She knew instantly that it was Amy's diary. She had seen Amy carry it enough times. It must have fallen out of her book bag the last time Amy was in her car.

Sara closed her eyes and held the diary between her palms. She took a deep breath and asked herself whether or not she should read it.

One side of her conscience told her that it would be all right. There could be something inside that would help her find out who killed Amy.

The other side of her conscience told her that it would be wrong to read what was inside. It was Amy's diary — a record of her own private thoughts. Now that she was dead, they were sacred.

If it helps me find her killer, then Amy would want me to read it, Sara thought. Perhaps it's even a sign of some sort that I found it at all.

Sara continued to hold the book between her palms without opening it. She pressed her lips together.

Finally, she decided on a test. If the diary was locked, she wouldn't try to open it. She would drive right to Amy's house and give it to her mother. But if the diary was unlocked, then she was meant to read it.

Sara took a deep breath and tried the clasp. It came easily undone. The diary was open for her. Sara turned on the overhead light. Hesitantly, she turned to the first page, promising herself that she would only read as much as she needed to in order to find some information about what had happened to Amy. She quickly thumbed through until she came to the final pages.

Seeing Amy's thoughts written in her handwriting sent a strange shiver through Sara's body. There were pages devoted to Mark, her feelings about him, and plenty about Mark's worry about the upcoming scholarship exam. As Sara kept reading she found that, indeed, Amy had cared for Mark as much as she said she had. He listens with his heart, Sara read, and wondered if it was really true, or if Amy had imagined it.

But Amy wasn't completely blinded by love. As the pages went on she began mentioning Mark's jealousy and his bad temper more and more often.

Soon, Amy was writing about another boy — Wayne Hansen. Color flamed into Sara's face as she read Amy's private thoughts about Wayne, her tales of their secret meetings. From the steamy and romantic passages that filled the pages, it was quite clear that Amy had been secretly involved with Wayne. In fact, it had been going on for quite a while before the snapshots were taken of them dancing together at Liz's party.

Near the time of Amy's death, they had been fighting. Wayne wanted Amy to break up with Mark, but Amy had refused. She would not break up with Mark until after the scholarship exam. Wayne was furious.

But was it enough to make him kill Amy? Sara didn't think so, but she remembered her father saying that besides trusting your instincts, you always had to be prepared for surprises. Likely or not, Wayne was a suspect.

Sara's brow furrowed. The last several pages of Amy's diary had been ripped out. What had she been so afraid of that she couldn't even keep in her diary?

A long sigh escaped Sara's lips. She would never know for sure. Amy had taken that knowledge with her to her grave.

Sara closed the diary and put it beside her on the seat. While she had been reading, evening had turned into night. Stars decorated the dark sky. Sara decided to take a drive up on the ridge along the Buckeye River. She wanted to take the diary to Amy's mother right away.

A maid ushered Sara into the Hendersens' dining room. Dr. Hendersen was seated at the gleaming mahogany table, pen and checkbook in hand, papers spread out in front of her. She was dressed in a pullover and torn jeans. For an instant Sara thought she was looking at Amy. She blinked.

Dr. Hendersen put down her pen. "Hello, Sara," she said. "It's nice to see you — and it's an excuse for me to take a break from paying bills. Sit down. Would you like something? Tea, perhaps, or some coffee?"

Sara shook her head. "No, thanks." She produced the diary from her pocket. "I found this in my car. It must have fallen out of Amy's book bag." She held the book out to Dr. Hendersen.

For a moment the woman held it in her hand and stared as if she didn't understand. Then a series of emotions moved across her face — comprehension, surprise, sadness, wonder. She held the diary close for a moment. "Thank you, Sara. It means so much to me."

Sara nodded. She read the unspoken question on Dr. Hendersen's face. She was wondering if Sara had read it. Perhaps she knew the answer, because she never voiced the question.

"Amy was such a romantic, Sara. She only wanted to see the best in people." Dr. Hendersen looked wistful. Then she smiled. "Not that she was easily fooled."

Sara had the feeling that Dr. Hendersen wasn't just talking. She was trying to tell her something, but she wasn't coming right out and saying it. For a moment she thought about asking what she meant. She didn't get the chance.

Suddenly the air was filled with a riot of flashing light. Panic gripped Sara. In her confusion she felt the impulse to run and to stand still at the same time. She gripped the back of a dining room chair tightly.

Dr. Hendersen's hands were pressed to her ears, her eyes squeezed shut. Sara could see the maid running down the staircase. She raced into the dining room, her face etched with fear. Gesturing wildly, she rushed to Dr. Hendersen.

After a moment Amy's mother touched Sara's shoulder. "It's the burglar alarm," she said, gesturing at the flashing lights. "The maid caught someone trying to break in upstairs."

## Chapter 10

**W**hoever had tried to break in was gone.
They had run away as soon as they had been
discovered. The maid was able to get that
much out, breathlessly, along with the fact
that she didn't get a good look at him. Then
she collapsed into the chair. One hand over
her heart, she closed her eyes.

Dr. Hendersen patted her on the shoulder
and told Sara she was going to turn off the
alarm. As soon as the lights stopped flashing,
the pounding of Sara's heart began to slow
down.

When Amy's mother returned, she explained that the alarm electronically notified
the police. They were probably already on
their way.

Dr. Hendersen was right. Barely a few minutes later, two uniformed officers arrived. Along with them was Sara's brother. The sight of him sent a shiver of curiosity through Sara.

The officers exchanged a few words with Amy's mother and then headed upstairs. Steve remained, asking questions and taking notes. Sara watched, wishing she could read their lips clearly.

Dr. Hendersen led Steve into the dining room. He did a double take when he saw Sara. "What are you doing here?" he demanded, the trace of anger on his face clearly implying that she shouldn't be.

Before Sara could answer, Dr. Hendersen spoke up. "She came to give me Amy's diary."

Steve turned to Sara with a questioning look.

*Found it. My car.* Sara signed sharply.

She read Dr. Hendersen's lips. "Amy took her diary everywhere. It must have dropped out of her book bag when Sara gave her a ride . . ." Dr. Hendersen stopped speaking abruptly. Sara filled in the missing words in her mind . . . the day Amy died.

"Wait here," Steve told Sara. He took Dr. Hendersen's arm and steered her out of the dining room and back into the foyer. Sara knew that Steve had deliberately turned their backs to her so that she wouldn't be able to read their lips. She folded her arms and watched with resentment.

Seconds ticked by, and the two of them remained deep in conversation. She checked over her shoulder as she edged toward the staircase. The maid was still sitting in the chair, eyes closed, a pained expression on her face.

Slowly, Sara crept up the staircase, then down the long, wide hallway. She knew the sound of her footsteps was muffled by the thick, ornate carpet under her feet.

She eased by each room, on the lookout for the two officers. Every room she passed was huge in comparison to her own room at home. Each was decorated with a matching set of gleaming mahogany furniture, thick carpets, and heavy, expensive draperies.

Nothing was the slightest bit out of place. There wasn't a speck of dust anywhere. It was all too sterile, too stiff, Sara thought. She preferred the casual feeling of the apartment she shared with Steve.

The officers were in a room at the end of the hall. Sara flattened herself beside the door, turned her head, and peered inside.

The two officers were studying a window at the back of the room. It was raised a few inches. There was a long, jagged crack in the glass.

Sara's eyes traveled over the room, taking in the contents. There were ballet posters on the wall and two bunches of dried flowers. She took a long breath as she saw a pair of shoes on the floor. Amy's shoes. This was Amy's room.

Sara watched the officers talking and gesturing, and pointing to the window. The one with a dark mustache took off his hat and scratched his head. The shorter one spread his arms in a puzzled gesture.

Sara backed away and went back downstairs. She knew what had happened. It wasn't that someone had wanted to break into the house. Specifically, the person wanted to break into Amy's room. There were expensive things to steal all over the house, but that wasn't what the burglar was after. Trying to enter through Amy's window didn't make any sense, and that was why the officers were puzzled.

Whoever it was wanted something that Amy had, and they wanted it badly enough that they couldn't wait until the dead of night when the employees had gone away and Dr. Hendersen was asleep.

When she returned to the dining room Sara was relieved to see the maid in the same position as when she had left, as if she had become a living statue. Dr. Hendersen and Steve were still talking when Sara entered the foyer. Her handsome brother's face was lit with the excitement that showed he had picked up a clue. Sara ached with curiosity that she didn't dare show.

"Sara, this might take a while. You should go on home and have some dinner. I'll see you later." Steve said it all very quickly, and turned eagerly back to Dr. Hendersen.

Sara knew it was useless to object. She tapped Steve on the arm to get his attention.

"Okay. Do you want me to save you some dinner?"

Steve shook his head, distracted, hardly paying attention. *Good-bye,* Sara signed to his back as she left.

It was after eight when Steve came home. "No dinner, I've got to work," was all he said to Sara before heading into the den. Through the door she could see him switch on the lamp and settle into her father's chair. He pulled a file out of his briefcase.

Steve saw her watching and his eyes flashed a warning that said, Don't ask what I'm working on. Don't keep standing there. Go away.

Sara left. She lay on her bed and stared up at the ceiling, thinking about the jagged crack in Amy's window and who could have put it there.

After half an hour she became restless and went to the kitchen for a snack. When she passed the den she peeked in. Steve had dozed off. The file he had been holding had slipped to the floor.

Sara's heart fluttered. She just had to see that file.

Step by step she tiptoed toward the den. At

the door she paused and watched her brother's chest gently rise and fall. Her pulse quickened.

Steve stirred in the chair. His body shifted and he scratched his ear.

Sara's heart sank. He was going to wake up. She had lost her chance. She trembled as she waited for his eyes to open.

They didn't. Steve settled back into the chair and stopped moving.

Once again, Sara started forward, tiptoeing. She scooped up the file and fingered the pages inside with shaking hands.

One look at the picture on top of the pile inside, and Sara gasped in shock, and turned her face away. It was a picture of Amy's body, lying by the edge of the pond. Sara closed her eyes and shoved it behind the other papers.

On top of the next page, Mark Royce's name jumped out at her. The document was the transcript of an interview between Mark and her brother. She remembered the intense look of recognition that had passed between them in Dr. Hendersen's house after the funeral. Now she understood why.

At the bottom of the page, Steve had written Mark's name in ballpoint pen, with a question mark after it. From the deep groove in the page she could tell that he had traced the name and the question mark over and over again.

Sara thumbed through the rest of the pages. There were notations about the time the body was found. Officers on a routine patrol had called in a report.

Sara's heart jumped into her throat. Mark Royce had been found beside the body.

Suddenly the file was ripped from Sara's hands. Steve put his face close to hers and cupped her chin tightly. "What are you doing?"

Sara jerked her head away, and began signing furiously. *Mark was found near Amy's body. He and Amy quarreled that day. He had a dangerous temper. Her death was no accident. Murder. Why haven't you arrested him?*

Steve brought the edge of his hand down against his palm. *Stop.* "Slow down, Sara," he said. "I can't follow when you sign so fast."

Sara took a deep breath. "I saw," she said, pointing to the file and the papers scattered on the floor. "You never thought Amy's death was an accident. Murder." She tapped her chest. "I know Mark Royce did it."

Steve put his head in his hands for a moment. When he looked up again, Sara thought the weariness on his face was deeper than before.

"All right, Sara, all right. We suspect that Amy was murdered."

"Mark was found near the body and he had a motive!" Sara didn't realize she had raised her voice until Steve raised his hands to his ears. Then he put his index finger against his lips. "Shhhh . . ."

He began to explain. "Mark told us someone called and told him Amy was in the park with another guy."

Sara shook her head. "Lies."

"No, Sara, maybe not. We know some people were aware of how jealous he was about Amy. Sometimes they played pranks — telling him she was seeing someone else — telephoning him. We talked to several students who admitted it, but none admitted calling that day. Phone records show there were two calls made from different pay phones to his house that evening."

Sara let this sink in. "He still could have lied." She threw her hands in the air. "Or maybe the person who made the prank call was the killer."

Steve got to his feet. "We are investigating all of the possibilities. If it really was murder — and we aren't absolutely sure that it was — we'll find the killer."

"Fine." Sara hoped the word came out as sarcastically as she meant it. "You should have told me."

"Now that you know — can you tell me anything that will help?"

"I already did. Mark Royce and Amy fought that day. He was jealous of Wayne Hansen." Sara paused. "Amy really was seeing Wayne. I read about it in her diary," she said haltingly.

Steve reached into his briefcase. Sara's eyes widened as he held up Amy's diary.

"Amy's mother gave this to me. She thought it might help in the investigation."

Sara could only stand and stare. "Why didn't anyone tell me . . ." she began.

A long sigh escaped Steve's lips. "I didn't want you to get involved, Sara. You always end up putting yourself in danger."

Steve's expression hardened. "I don't want you playing detective this time. I can't conduct this investigation and be worrying about your safety. If I find out you've been snooping in any way, I'll keep you at home. You won't even leave the house to go to school. I mean it."

Steve began stuffing papers into the briefcase. "I'd better get this stuff back to the station. I don't want to leave temptation lying around."

Sara was stunned. She could only stand and watch as Steve put on his coat and walked out the door.

On the way out, he passed Keesha in the hall. She was on her way over.

*I thought you had a date,* Sara signed.

*I did,* Keesha signed back. *But the poor guy had such a bad cold that I finally told him to go home.* She smiled. *I think I'll give him another chance, though. He's nice.*

*That's good.* Sara couldn't really focus on Keesha's dating story. *I've got a cold, too.* Sara inhaled, and was surprised that she didn't feel stuffed up any more. *On second thought, maybe it's been shocked out of me.*

Keesha looked at her intently. *Okay. Tell me what happened.*

Quickly, Sara filled Keesha in on everything — finding Amy's diary, the attempted break-in, and what she had just discovered in Steve's file.

Keesha didn't say anything. She didn't make a move to sign.

*Well?* Sara prompted.

Keesha's fingers moved. *A lot has happened today. I think you should take a break from it all. Let's get pizza, hang out, maybe watch a movie.*

Sara realized that what Keesha said made sense. Her mind was reeling with details and suspicions whirling around and around. She knew she couldn't figure anything out tonight.

*You're right. Sausage and mushroom pizza, okay?*

*Fine. I'll go pick it up. They take forever to deliver.*

*I'll come with you.*

*No. You stay here and try to calm down. You're wound up so tight you look like you could take off and fly.*

Sara had to laugh. Keesha had a way of speaking her mind.

*Good to see you laughing. I'll be right back.*

Maybe it would have been better to wait for the delivery after all, Keesha thought as she waved good-bye to the doorman and stepped out into the night. The temperature had dropped since she came in from her date. She pulled the cap on her head down over her ears.

Keesha left the brightly lit area around Thurston Court and turned down a dimly lit, tree-lined street that led to the Pizza Palace. She hoped that Sara was watching television or doing something else to take her mind off the murder investigation. She was so tense it was no wonder that she was sick.

Keesha could see the lights of the Pizza Palace up ahead. She didn't like this stretch of road in between. It was too dark and too quiet.

Something moved in the shadows by the side of the road. It's nothing, Keesha told herself, but she began walking faster.

Was that sound behind her footsteps? She wasn't sure. She sped up her pace.

The wind blew the lid off a garbage can and sent it clattering down the street. Keesha could hardly stand the suspense. She stood still for a moment, listening. No footsteps.

Reeeowww! A cat shot out in front of her, its hair standing up along its back. Keesha jumped, and her heart began pounding in her chest. In an instant, she realized her mistake and began to laugh at her fear.

She stood still, out of breath. Her hand was pressed to her chest and her lips curved into a smile at her own foolishness. It's all this talk about murder that has me spooked, she thought.

Keesha started walking again, determined not to let her mind play tricks on her or to let her imagination get carried away. When she heard the rustling in the dry branches of the bushes by the side of the road, she told herself it was just the wind.

Then she heard the unmistakable sound of footsteps — heavy and uneven. Step — scrape — step — scrape. As she quickened her own pace, the steps behind her sped up, faster and faster. Step, scrape, step, scrape, stepscrapestepscrapestep.

Keesha knew someone was coming after her. It was no trick of her imagination. Now she knew real, deep, soul-chilling fear.

Keesha ran, the awful noise of her pursuer's steps echoing in her ears. The steps were getting closer.

Her voice froze in her throat as she felt a strong hand grip her arm and whirl her around. She gazed into dark eyes in a face hidden behind a black ski mask.

Whoever it was straightened up suddenly and dropped her arm. He stepped backward awkwardly. Then he turned and ran away in a clumsy, one-sided shuffle.

# Chapter 11

*What happened?* Sara signed with alarm as Keesha came racing back into the apartment.

Keesha began talking, her words spilling out in a torrent.

Sara brought the edge of her hand down against her other palm. *Stop,* she signed. *You're talking too fast.*

Keesha held both hands in front of her chest, palms up, and wiggled her fingers. *Wait.* She sank into a chair and took several deep breaths. She ran a hand along her forehead.

Sara waited, tense and fearful. She had never seen Keesha so shaken. Whatever had happened to make her this way must have been very frightening.

Finally Keesha began signing. Her fingers fluttered as she poured out her story.

*I wonder if it's the same guy that came after me by the library,* Sara signed when she finished.

Keesha signed back, *Whoever it was they weren't after just anybody.* She pointed to her coat. *I put your coat and hat on because I didn't want to go to my apartment to get mine. They were after you.*

An hour after the incident, Marisa Douglas sat behind the desk outside the Emergency Room at East End General Hospital and rubbed her tired eyes. Since her boyfriend Steve Howell said he would be working overtime on a case, she had decided to take advantage of her free Saturday night to catch up on some paperwork. It wasn't her idea of a fun evening, but things had been so busy lately that she'd gotten seriously bogged down.

Marisa rubbed her tapered hands together.

The hospital was so quiet at this time of night. Visiting hours were over, the nurses had finished their rounds until the next shift. Most of the patients were sleeping. The phones weren't even ringing. It was the perfect time to work without distractions.

Marisa stood up and stretched. She glanced at her watch and yawned. If she put in another hour, she'd be able to have everything squared away for Monday. She decided a cup of coffee would get her through the hour.

The cafeteria was closed. She'd have to get the coffee from the vending machine. A grimace of distaste flickered over her finely sculpted features. The vending machine coffee was terrible. Marisa gave a little shudder. It was that or nothing, and she needed coffee.

Marisa grabbed some change from her purse, then put it back in the cabinet and locked it. Her shoes squeaked on the slick tile floor as she walked toward the vending area.

Her thoughts turned to Steve, and her lips curved in a gentle smile. They had been growing closer lately. Because their schedules made it difficult for them to spend as much time together as they wanted, they made sure they made the most out of every minute.

Steve had been working so hard. He had already had a full caseload, and then took on this murder investigation, too. Marisa knew how he threw himself into his work, and she hoped it wouldn't be much longer before he could take a break. He worked so hard that he exhausted himself. Plus, because the victim was a friend of Sara's, he worried even more than usual about her becoming involved.

Marisa tucked a strand of hair behind her ear. Sometimes she thought Steve worried too much about Sara. She was older than he realized. But she knew he felt a great deal of pressure to do everything right for her.

At the vending machine Marisa deposited two quarters and pressed the selection with milk, no sugar. Her mouth puckered as she imagined the strong, too sharp taste.

The coffee poured into the cup, followed by a dollop of powdered creamer. Marisa opened the little plastic window and lifted the cup. She stirred with a plastic stirrer as she walked back to the desk.

Marisa had gone about halfway down the hall when she paused. There were voices coming from inside the room beside her. Actually, it was just one voice, she realized. She stopped and listened.

It was a man's voice. He was agitated, angry.

"Why couldn't you just get the negatives back? Why did you get scared all of a sudden when you found out Amy was dead? You shouldn't have tried to run. I knew you'd tell everything if you got picked up. I thought I had stopped you, too, by having that boulder thrown through your windshield. This time I'll really stop you."

Alarmed, Marisa pushed open the door. The room had two beds, with a partition between them. One bed was empty. Whoever she heard speaking was standing on the other side of the partition.

The light from the street threw his shadow on the wall, magnifying it so that it reached nearly to the ceiling. Marisa gasped. She could see the outline of a pillow in his hand. He was bending over the patient.

"Hey!" she called sharply. "You aren't supposed to be in here. I'm calling hospital security."

Marisa screamed as the partition came tumbling down on her. Before she could push it away, someone ran from the room. She heard the sound of running footsteps in the hall.

Marisa hurried to the door and looked out. The man was gone. She didn't even get a glimpse of him.

She let out an explosive burst of breath. She'd tell security. First, she'd find out if the patient knew who it was.

"Hello?" Marisa said softly as she bent over the man lying there. One look at him, plus a quick perusal of his chart told her that she wouldn't be getting any information from the man. His name was Charles Dolan. He was in a coma.

"It looks like Charlie Dolan was mixed up somehow in Amy's murder," Steve told Sara when she awoke the next morning. He was holding a glass of orange juice. Sara took one look at his face and realized he'd been up all night.

"Marisa called me from the hospital a little after eleven last night," he said. "It looks like somebody was thinking about finishing off Dolan."

Sara interrupted. "Did she see who it was?"

Steve shook his head. "No. Not at all. It's too bad." Steve took a sip of juice. "Anyway, you can see why I don't want you messing around and getting involved. Whoever is mixed up in this is dangerous." He let out a yawn. "I'm going to take a nap, then it's back to work." He touched the side of Sara's face. "I'm sorry. Once this is over we'll spend more time together."

Sara signed as she said, "*I'd like that.*"

Wearily, Steve pushed himself out of his chair. "Later," he said, and headed to the bedroom. He turned around. "Sara, Marisa heard whoever was in Dolan's room talking about negatives. Have you heard anything like that at school?"

Sara studied Steve's face. She held her breath and shook her head.

Steve shrugged. "Well, I suppose I'm glad to hear it." He turned his back and continued down the hall.

When the door closed, Sara let out her breath. *I probably should have told him about the phone call Keesha got, demanding the negatives,* she thought. *But I couldn't. He might keep me out of school, or have me trailed. I couldn't stand that.*

Sara was pouring cornflakes into her bowl when she saw the light of the TTY flashing in the den. She hurried to answer it. Her heart beat faster when she realized it was Bret. He missed her and he wanted to see her that night.

Sara missed him too. She didn't hesitate before she typed, **Yes**.

That evening, Sara's heart leaped as she saw Bret's car. She said good night to the doorman and hurried outside.

*It's so good to see you, Sara,* Bret touched her cheek as soon as she got into the car.

*It's good to see you, too.*

Bret leaned toward her, then pulled back as he saw John O'Connor.

Bret drove around to the back of the building and pulled under some trees. He and Sara reached for each other at the same time. They clung to each other. Then Bret pressed his mouth on Sara's.

Sara raised her hands to the back of his neck and tangled her fingers in his hair. She loved the closeness of him, loved feeling the softness of his hair, the roughness of his jacket, loved the smell of his aftershave.

Bret kissed her again. Sara tilted her head back and breathed deeply. A delicious, tingling warmth swept through her. She slid her hands over his shoulders. He caressed her hair.

Sara pulled back and looked into his eyes. Her face felt warm. "I think we'd better go," she said.

Bret's eyes were shining. "I suppose we'd better," he said.

They drove to a new place in downtown Radley that had already become a popular hangout. It was called The Blue Onion, and featured twenty-seven kinds of burgers.

The place was packed when they entered. People sat at long ranch-style wooden tables talking and laughing. Waiters and waitresses hurried back and forth from the kitchen, carrying trays of hamburgers.

Bret steered Sara away from the long wooden tables to a row of booths along the wall. *More privacy,* he signed.

*Good,* Sara signed back.

*I kept picturing your face in my mind, Sara,* Bret signed as they sat down.

Sara squeezed his hand gently and then signed back, *I hope we don't fight anymore.*

The waitress came, and they decided to go for two Blue Onion Specials — burgers with everything, and two Cokes.

As they waited for the burgers to arrive, Bret turned serious. *I don't want to fight either. It's just that I care so much for you I don't want anything to happen to you. When you put yourself in danger, I worry.*

I can't help it, Sara thought. It's part of who I am. When something happens to someone close to me, I can't just sit back and let someone else get involved.

Sara searched Bret's face. She held her words. Not tonight, she thought. I won't do anything to spoil tonight. But it was hard not to tell Bret all the things that were on her mind. She searched for something to say.

*I miss the way we used to dance in your basement,* she signed. Bret would turn the volume of the stereo up high, so that Sara could feel the vibrations through the floorboards. Then they would jump to the beat, or hold each other close and sway to the rhythm of the slow tunes.

*We'll dance together soon,* Bret signed.

The door opened and three guys entered. Two of them were tall, muscular and big-boned. The third was a little shorter, but just as muscularly built. Sara snapped up straighter in her chair as she recognized two of them — Mark Royce and Wayne Hansen.

Those two usually act like mortal enemies, she thought, her senses on alert. Why are they buddies all of a sudden? And who is the third guy with the nasty curl to his lip?

Bret tapped her on the arm. *What's wrong?*

Sara spread her fingers as she brought her hand forward from her chin. *Nothing.* She signed her reply without looking at Bret. She kept her eyes on the three boys.

The one she didn't recognize was as tall as

Mark, with broad shoulders, blond hair, and an insolent, jutting chin. There was something familiar about him, but it was just out of reach.

The big blond boy walked behind the other two. His gait was heavy, clumsy. Step, step, lurch. Step, step, lurch. Sara's breath caught in her throat. She knew that walk. Not only was his walk clumsy, he was limping.

Keesha's story about her attacker's uneven footsteps flashed into Sara's mind. She raised her hand to her mouth.

Sara knew without a doubt that she was looking at the person who had attacked her near the library a few nights ago, and the same person who had jumped Keesha last night.

# Chapter 12

It was all Sara could do to sit still while the blond boy was in the restaurant. Sara had the urge to run up to him and hit him — hard.

From the looks of him, he wouldn't have felt a thing. His jaw was as heavy as a cement block.

Sara's stomach twisted into knots as she tried to pay attention to Bret. He knew something was wrong and it cast a dull shadow over their bright reconciliation. He asked Sara what it was, but she denied that anything was the matter.

When Sara's burger came she could hardly eat it. She had to force herself to chew, swallow, chew, swallow. Each mouthful tasted like sawdust.

Bret dropped Sara off early. *I know you're hiding something,* he signed as he pulled to a stop at Thurston Court. *What is it?*

Sara looked down into her lap for a long time before she signed back. *You'll be angry if I tell you, and angry if I don't.* She looked at Bret sadly as she scrunched her fingers in front of her face. *Angry.*

An icy chill settled in Sara's heart when she saw the expression in Bret's eyes. She had never seen him look at her that way — cold, empty, and distant.

*I don't know how much more of this I can take, Sara. You worry me too much.*

What does he mean? Sara asked herself. Is he saying he wants to break up? Don't let it be that, she wished silently. She held her breath, a knife-edge of pain poised above her heart, waiting to strike.

Bret's hands jabbed the air, giving an angry edge to his signing. *Don't you understand how much I care for you? You keep putting yourself in danger and I can't make you stop.*

Sara felt tears beginning to well up in her eyes. She turned her face away from Bret.

After a moment he put his hand under her chin. Gently, he turned her face toward him.

*I can't leave you, either. You mean too much to me.* Bret looked deeply into her eyes. *I don't know what to do.* He kissed her softly, barely brushing her lips with his own. *I have to go now, Sara.*

The following Monday was a school holiday. Normally Sara would have spent it with Bret, but today her hand stopped as she started to call him on the TTY.

She wasn't exactly sure how things had been left between them. Bret said he couldn't leave her, yet he had said good-bye so abruptly that it felt that he had broken up with her after all.

Nothing was sure between them except that they still cared deeply for each other. Whether that was enough to keep them together, Sara didn't know.

Her heart ached, but she decided she couldn't call Bret. She had to let things be for now.

She knew what she should do that day. She was way behind on her history project. Day after day, she found excuses not to work on it. It brought back memories of Amy. Now, she decided, was the time to separate the work from those memories.

Sara sat down at her desk and began to write. Her pen scratched across the paper. It was nearly out of ink. If possible, Sara always did her homework with one kind of pen, fine tip blue. She decided that she'd have to have a new one before she got started on her work.

As she dressed in jeans and a sweater, she knew that she was finding another excuse to put off her work. But she promised herself she would go to the stationery store, and not stop anywhere else. Then she would come right home.

As soon as she got downtown, however, Sara found reason after reason to break her promise to herself. When she passed the drugstore, she remembered they were low on toothpaste. Inside, she couldn't resist lingering in the aisle where makeup was displayed.

On the way out of the drugstore, she spotted a pair of jeans she liked in the boutique across the street. Even though she didn't bring much money with her, she decided to try them on anyway.

Then, as she was leaving the boutique, she bumped into Wayne Hansen. He flashed her a wide smile.

Sara stopped short. Her confusion must have showed on her face, because after a moment Wayne's smile faded.

"I saw you with Mark Royce yesterday," Sara said.

Wayne's smile returned. "Things have been kind of rocky between us lately — but we go way back. We both grew up on the docks."

Sara straightened up and blinked.

"Yeah, it's kind of rough over there," Wayne said as if he had read her mind. "My family moved when I was ten."

Sara could see why Amy had found Wayne so appealing. Compared to Mark's moody, volatile disposition, Wayne's open, sunny manner must have been a welcome change. He was good-looking, too, with a square jaw, medium brown hair, and dark eyes. Even under his heavy jacket she could see the muscles of his biceps.

"How about your other friend, the blond boy you were at The Blue Onion with last night? Was he from the docks too?" Sara tried to make the question casual.

Wayne knitted his brows. "Oh, Bobby? As a matter of fact, he was. We just bumped into him as we were going in." Uncertainty flickered in his eyes. "Why all the questions?"

Words came out of Sara's mouth before she knew what she was saying. "I know about you and Amy," she blurted.

The smile vanished. Wayne's expression darkened, and he clenched his jaw. Whatever was open and sunny about him had gone away, leaving a grim, angry stranger in its place.

"Mind your own business, Sara," was all he said before he walked away.

Sara watched him go. She had never seen Wayne act that way. The change had come over him so suddenly. Why did he want to hide his involvement with Amy now — unless he had something else to hide?

Sara mulled over what had just happened as she walked toward Andy's Stationery Store. She had hoped Wayne would open up to her. Now she thought he would avoid talking to her again.

There was something very satisfying about the sight of row upon row of notebooks, pads, and pens inside Andy's Stationery. *Hi,* she signed to the owner, who was behind the cash register.

Andy returned the signed greeting. The corners of his green eyes crinkled behind his glasses. He introduced Sara to the new clerk he was breaking in, a wiry fellow of medium height, with shoulder-length dark hair. "Sara, meet Ralph."

Ralph squinted as he watched Sara move her fingers as she spoke. *"Hi, Ralph."*

"She's deaf?" he asked, with a sidelong glance at Andy.

"Ask me," Sara said. "I can read lips. I understand you."

Ralph spoke very slowly, exaggerating each word. "It's wonderful you're out all by yourself."

Sara twisted the corner of her mouth and looked at Andy. He rolled his eyes.

"You've got a lot to learn, Ralph," he said.

He clapped him on the shoulder. "Get out there and help some customers," he said.

"Uh, but I'm new," Ralph stammered.

"Go, go, go," said Andy, giving him a slight shove. Andy flipped his hand disgustedly in the air in Ralph's direction. He drew a circle around his heart. "That means 'sorry,' right?"

Sara nodded. *"That's okay. Not your fault."* She looked on the counter where he usually kept a supply of her favorite pens. She shook her head and raised her eyebrows questioningly. She pointed to the container where the pens were kept.

Andy understood immediately. "You want the Aqualine."

Sara nodded.

Andy looked as if he was doing some mental head scratching. Then he snapped his fingers. "They came in but we didn't bring 'em upstairs yet." A man approached the counter and asked for help. Andy motioned for him to wait.

"I'm too busy to leave the floor now, Sara," he said. "But they're right at the bottom of the stairs." He pointed to a door at the rear of the store. "Right through there. You can get some yourself, but be careful going down the steps."

Sara smiled and nodded. She went to the back of the store and opened the door that was marked "Employees only."

The stairway that led to the floor below was narrow and lit with a single unshaded bulb. Sara tightly gripped the length of pipe that served as a handrail as she descended step by step.

At the bottom of the stairs, pads and calendars were stacked in one corner. On top of them Sara found several boxes marked "Aqualine" with the familiar blue fish on them. She picked up two boxes. As she turned to go, something caught her eye. It was a stack of ruled notebook paper, but in light violet instead of white. That could make taking notes more interesting, she thought.

The door at the top of the stairs opened. Sara felt vibrations grow stronger and stronger as a figure descended the stairs. She turned to look up, expecting to see Andy. Her heart froze as she saw a figure dressed in black, his face hidden behind a black ski mask. He came toward her.

Sara wanted to run, but fear kept her rooted to the spot, kept her from opening her mouth and making a sound. Her terror mounted as she recognized the clumsy, lurching gait as the figure reached out for her.

In an instant, her purse was pulled from her arm and she felt herself being shoved roughly into a storeroom. The door slammed shut behind her, plunging her into darkness. Now she could not hear, and she could not see.

Her hands groped for the doorknob, but she couldn't find it. Blood surged through her veins. She could feel it rushing through her head. Now she was a prisoner in the void that seemed to close over her as if she was in a coffin.

# Chapter 13

Sara didn't know how long she had been in the deep, silent darkness, when finally the door of the storeroom opened. Then Andy was bending over her. His lips were moving. Sara forced herself to concentrate. He wanted to know if she was all right.

Slowly, Sara pushed herself into a sitting position. She raised her hand to her mouth as if she were holding a cup and drinking. "Water," Andy said hurriedly. "I'll get some."

He disappeared for a moment and returned holding a paper cup. Sara drank deeply. She ran her tongue around her mouth. It felt like she would be able to talk.

"What happened?" Andy asked.

Sara shrugged. "Someone grabbed me. Took my purse."

Andy knitted his brows. "The stuff you had in your purse is scattered all over outside the storeroom. He held out her wallet. "There is still cash in it," he said. "If this guy didn't want to steal anything, what was he after?"

Sara shook her head weakly, although she was pretty sure he was looking for some negatives. She couldn't explain the whole thing to Andy, anyway. Slowly, she got to her feet. "Did you see anybody go running out of the store? Someone dressed in black, and wearing a ski mask?"

Andy shook his head. "No, but the store was crowded. Are you sure you're okay? Do you want me to call your brother?"

"No!" Sara blurted out. She put on her coat. "I'll be fine."

Andy handed Sara her purse. "Here. I gathered up all your things. Take these too," he added. "No charge." Andy held out two boxes of Aqualine pens, and the paper Sara had picked out.

"Thanks," she said, and left.

It wasn't until she got home that Sara discovered the note her attacker had left in her coat pocket. She stared at the scrawled, misshapen letters and realized he must have used one of the pens she had gone downstairs to get.

The note was an angry demand for some negatives. The instructions were to put them in an envelope and leave them behind the *Motorcycle Driver* magazines at Rudy's News by 6:00 that evening. It ended by threatening that if she didn't do as she was told, "what happened to Amy will happen to you."

Sara took off her coat and walked into the bathroom. Her hair was messed up and there was a streak of dirt on her cheek. Besides that, and a bruise on her arm, she was all right — so far, she thought. She turned on the faucet.

This whole thing — Amy's death, Charlie Dolan's accident, the attacks and threats were all about some negatives. Sara was surprised that the threatening note had made her more angry than scared.

What negatives? What negatives? she

asked herself as she scrubbed at the dirt on her face.

The light in the hallway blinked. Sara turned and saw Steve's hand on the switch. *Hi*, he signed.

Steve still had dark circles under his eyes, but otherwise he looked more rested than he had in days. She soon understood why.

"I fell asleep at my desk," Steve said, grinning sheepishly. "Lt. Marino found me. I was out for hours."

I almost was too, Sara thought. It was probably what her attacker had in mind when he hit her.

"I just came home to shower and change clothes," Steve said. "I'm sorry I've been away so much. We'll spend more time together soon. I've just got to wrap up this case."

Sara smiled and nodded. Her insides tightened. She wanted to tell him everything — about the threats, the attacks, the note.

The impulse was fleeting. Sara rejected it immediately. Once Steve heard she had been attacked, he would be so upset that at the very least he would have her trailed constantly. He might even try to keep her from leaving the apartment. She didn't think posting a guard at the door was beyond him.

"Something the matter?" Steve asked.

Hurriedly, Sara shook her head. She glanced at her watch and pretended to suddenly notice the lateness of the hour. "Downtown. School supplies," she said hurriedly.

Steve looked as if he was hardly paying attention. There was a preoccupied look on his face. She knew he was thinking about the case.

"Fine," he said, glancing at her before he turned around and headed toward his room.

Sara's thoughts returned to the problem of the negatives. The only connection her mind made was with the pictures from Liz Martinson's party — the ones that showed Wayne and Amy dancing together. Those pictures were still in her locker. There was no way she could get into school and get them now.

No matter, Sara decided. She didn't want to give up those negatives anyway. They might contain a clue that would help unravel the mystery surrounding Amy's death.

Sara hurried to her room and opened her

photo album. She rifled through the negatives she had stashed in envelopes in the back. She found some she had taken at school years ago, when they had taken a trip to the circus. She pulled them out of the album and stuffed them in an envelope. She put on her coat and snapped on Tuck's leash, then unsnapped it again. She didn't want to be conspicuous as she waited to see who claimed the envelope at Rudy's. Tuck's presence there would be like wearing a neon sign.

Steve liked Sara to take Tuck with her when she went out alone in the evening. Sara glanced down the hall. The bathroom door was closed. Steve was probably in the shower.

She waved a quick good-bye to Tuck, and hurried out the door.

At Rudy's, she slid the envelope into the last *Motorcycle Driver* magazine, at the very back of the stack. She moved behind a pillar not far away, and waited. It was 5:45. Who-ever wanted the negatives might already be there, watching her. She hoped they wanted the negatives badly enough to come and get them right in front of her.

The store closed early, at 7:00. Sara was prepared to stay until the last minute to catch her suspect.

Sara studied the crowd. There was the usual bunch of boys, junior high school age and younger, near the rack of comic books. A young woman about Steve's age was looking through a bridal magazine. Another girl with a cast on her arm and a bandage on her leg was looking through the science section.

The girl turned to the side. Sara drew her breath in sharply. It was Karen Lee, one of the scholarship candidates at school. She hurried toward her.

Karen saw Sara out of the corner of her eye and smiled.

"What happened?" Sara asked.

Karen shook her head. "I don't know much. I was riding my bicycle and some-one rode by and pushed me, hard. I fell off the bike and got pretty banged up." She shrugged. "I'm okay now. It's a good thing I broke my right hand instead of my left. I'm left-handed, so I won't have any trouble fill-ing in the answer sheet at the exam."

"When is the exam?"

Karen's eyes widened in surprise. "Tomorrow! Sara, where have you been? Everyone is talking about it!"

Sara stammered something about having a lot on her mind. The words "good luck" formed on her lips, but she never got them out. The sight of Karen's shocked expression stopped her. The girl's jaw dropped and she jerked her head toward the front of the store.

Sara looked and saw the woman throw the bridal magazine into the air. Next to her, a revolving rack holding paperback books was toppling over. All the customers, including Karen, were running to the front of the store.

The clerk, a baby-faced doughy fellow, jumped from behind the counter and streaked out to the sidewalk.

Sara started to follow, when she saw a sight that made her heart sink. The stack of *Motorcycle Driver* magazines lay scattered over the floor. Before she looked for the envelope, she already knew it was gone.

## Chapter 14

*Stupid.* Sara hit her forehead with the heel of her hand. She had allowed herself to be distracted while she was talking to Karen, and had taken her eyes off the magazines. It had only been for a few minutes, but it had cost her a look at her suspect.

Who was it, and how did the person get away so fast? she wondered. She pictured the tall, big-boned boy who had attacked her before. It seemed impossible that he could have entered the store without her noticing.

Huffing and puffing, the clerk dragged back into the store. An expression of disgust was etched on his baby-faced features.

Sara hurried toward him. "Did you get a good look at who you were chasing?"

The clerk grimaced. "Good enough to recognize him if he comes in again. Little twerp. The boy's only about ten years old and he's already stealing." The clerk shook his head. His expression showed that he thought the shoplifter's future had already been decided, and it wasn't good.

A ten-year-old boy, Sara repeated to herself. She was stunned. Somehow, she had stumbled into an awful coincidence. The magazine was gone, but the wrong person took it.

Clearly the ten-year-old boy wasn't the one who had slipped the threatening note into her pocket. He had lifted the magazine because he wanted it — not the envelope inside.

Sara looked around the store. Only two boys remained, looking at comic books. Where was the person who had wanted the negatives, and what would he do when he realized he wasn't going to get them?

The baby-faced clerk trudged toward her. "Can I help you find something?"

Sara shook her head.

Baby-face didn't move. "I'm closing up

early tonight." He glanced at his watch in a way that clearly showed that Sara was taking up his valuable time. For an instant he regarded her with undisguised suspicion, no doubt because of his recent theft. After a moment he turned and went back behind the cash register, where he sat staring resentfully, drumming his fingers on the counter.

There wasn't much point in staying any longer, Sara thought. As she left she nodded to the clerk, being more polite than she thought he deserved. He nodded back sullenly. She could feel his eyes following her as she walked toward her car.

Though the sky was dark, the streetlights and store signs blazed brightly and the sidewalks were crowded with people. Still, Sara looked nervously to the right and left, glancing over her shoulder now and then. She couldn't help feeling that someone was about to leap out at her.

In her car, she sat at the curb, unable to decide where to go. She wished Keesha was there to confide in. Still, she thought, although it would be comforting to share her thoughts, what could Keesha do?

Sara sighed. Perhaps now was the time to tell Steve everything, she thought. She would show him the threatening note and pour out everything that had happened. It was too dangerous to keep it to herself any longer. Yes, she decided, telling Steve was the right thing to do.

Sara pulled the car away from the curb and turned in the direction of the precinct. The downtown traffic was light. People must be settling down after the long weekend, getting ready to go back to work and to school, she decided.

At a stoplight Sara watched a boy and girl her own age cross in front of her. They were arm in arm, their heads close together as they shared their laughter. She looked at them wistfully and thought of Bret.

She eased the car onto Harrison Street. Soon the lights of the station were in sight. As it got closer and closer, Sara felt her chest tightening.

What would Steve say when he discovered she had been hiding things from him? What would he do?

Steve was tired from overwork, his nerves

stretched taut already. Sara pictured what could be another terrible scene between them, her brother's eyes flashing, his face clouded with rage.

Sara's car was in front of the station. A couple of guys that Steve rotated shifts with waved. A parking spot beckoned to her.

You're in the fix you're in because you kept so many secrets from Steve for so long, she told herself. The more you wait, the worse telling him will be — not to mention the danger you may be in. Get it over with.

Sara slowed down. She wondered if her brother would ever trust her again. Her insides churned the way they did when she was in the doctor's office and saw the needle before a blood test. Her hands gripped the steering wheel tightly.

Sara never pulled the car to a stop. She pressed her foot on the accelerator and kept going. The police station grew smaller and smaller in her rearview mirror.

I can't tell him, Sara thought miserably. I can't. She drove on, turning down one street, then another, her thoughts jumbled and confused.

When she saw the sign for the Side Door Café, she realized that her route hadn't been so aimless after all. It was no accident that she had ended up close to Bret's house.

She decided that she would drive past his house, but that she wouldn't try to speak to him. She had to be near him somehow. She pulled her car onto the road that went by the faculty housing.

When she passed Bret's house, however, disappointment settled like a lump in her stomach. No one was home. The house was dark.

Sara felt hollow inside. Instead of going back through the streets she decided to go back home on the expressway that ran just outside Radley. She would get home faster that way. Then she would go and see Keesha.

She glanced up just in time to see the red glow of the light as she went through it. Careful, she told herself. She remembered not so long ago when she was so preoccupied she almost rear-ended another car.

Sara sped up as she headed onto the expressway. She enjoyed the open feeling of the road, and being able to go on and on without stopping. There were several car lengths between her and the vehicle in front of her.

Sara breathed deeply and watched the scenery whizzing by. For the short time that she was on this road, she didn't have to think about anything — not the murder investigation, or threats, or problems with Steve or Bret. Sara tried to free her mind from thoughts of anything but the road ahead.

She was quickly approaching the car ahead. Why are some people so poky on an open road like this one? she asked herself as she eased into the next lane. Soon she left the car behind.

Sara drew beside another car, then quickly left it behind as well. It happened with two more cars, one after the other.

Take it easy, she told herself as she headed onto the downhill portion of the road. The speedometer edged higher and higher. Sara pressed her foot on the brake.

Nothing happened. For a moment Sara had the strange sensation that she had made a mistake, and hadn't really stepped on the brake after all. She'd only thought about it. She whizzed by another car.

There was a turn coming up. To the right of the turn was a brick wall. If she couldn't slow down, she wouldn't make the turn and would sail right into the wall.

All this flashed through Sara's mind as she frantically pumped the brake pedal. She was passing cars one after the other, so fast that she was having to weave from lane to lane.

The turn was coming closer and closer. Sara wanted to close her eyes and pray, but of course she didn't dare. She felt a dizzying, sickening wave of terror when the car tilted sharply as it whipped around the curve.

For an instant Sara was riding on only two wheels. Her heart hung suspended in her chest as she waited to topple over. Instead, the car shot out of the turn and the outside wheels hit the asphalt with a jolt as Sara wrenched the wheel.

The car straightened out and continued speeding down the incline. Traffic thickened as the road narrowed toward the intersection. It was becoming harder and harder to turn the wheel. It was like being on an amusement park ride that had gone suddenly and horribly out of control.

Sara fought to keep from losing herself in panic. Up ahead, cars swerved crazily to get out of her way. Faster, faster, faster, she went, the world racing by in a blur as she dodged car after car.

When she crashed, would it hurt terribly, or would everything simply go blank? Sara barely had time to wonder. At the intersection, just seconds away, an oil tanker was pulling directly across her path.

## Chapter 15

SELVANE. The letters on the side of the oil tanker's long metal drum loomed closer and closer. Sara had a blinding vision of the two vehicles colliding, of being engulfed in a hot blast of orange flame. Closer, closer, closer she came — the impact would happen any second.

Desperately, Sara wrenched the steering wheel to the right with all her strength. The car spun crazily, and smashed through the metal barrier at the side of the highway. Sara held on, the seat belt digging painfully into her stomach as the car bounced over the bumps on the shoulder of the road.

In an instant the speeding car cleared the

shoulder and was rocketing over the field that stretched beyond. Sara's palms burned as she jerked the steering wheel right and left to avoid smashing into trees.

After what seemed like forever, the car began to slow down. Then, in what seemed to Sara like a miracle, it stopped.

Sara leaned her head against the steering wheel and gave thanks that she was safe. Her heart was hammering so hard she feared it would burst through her chest.

She twisted around and looked behind her toward the expressway below. The headlights of the cars twinkled as they streamed past in lines.

Sara knew she had been incredibly lucky. The ground on the side of the expressway sloped upward gradually. It was the incline that had slowed and eventually stopped the car. She had come within a hair's breath of being killed.

Her hands trembled as she punched in the number of the towing service on her portable TTY. Thankfully, there was one in Radley that had a TTY. She typed in her location, and a moment later the operator typed back a response. They were sending someone out to her immediately.

Sara signed off the TTY. Now there was nothing to do but wait. Now that the ordeal was over, she felt drained, too weak to move.

She gazed up at the bare branches of the trees that looked like skeleton's hands reaching into the starry canopy overhead. A smoky cloud billowed across the sky and a fingernail moon emerged from behind it. Only a few yards away the machines of civilization sped by, but in this spot everything was so quiet, so still, as if she was miles from everything. Sara breathed deeply, thankful to be alive.

Moments later a flashing red-and-blue light announced the arrival of the tow truck. Though the driver didn't sign, he had been informed that she was deaf. He paid close attention as she explained what happened as clearly and with as few words as possible.

"We'll check it out," he said, before hooking up her car to the tow truck. "Sounds like a hole in your brake line. You didn't have any brake fluid left." The man made a motion as if he was washing his hands. "No fluid, no brakes. I bet that's what happened." He looked at the car and shook his head. "You're one lucky lady."

When they reached the garage, a mechanic confirmed what the tow truck driver suspected. There were two big holes slashed in her brake line. The mechanic, a wiry man with thinning gray hair and a lined, weathered faced looked alarmed as he told Sara, "We've got to report this to the police. This was no accident. No question about it, this was a deliberate crime. You could have been killed."

Sara nodded. She had already decided as much. As she had sat waiting in the office she had forced herself to think about what happened. She came to the conclusion that no matter what the outcome was, things had gotten too dangerous to keep them to herself.

The towing company arranged for someone to drive Sara home, and even contacted her brother for her. When she was dropped off at Thurston Court, Sara looked up at her window. She could see Steve's silhouette as he paced back and forth. She took a deep breath as she went inside the building.

"Sara!" Steve cried thankfully as she opened the apartment door. In an instant he rushed toward her and threw his arms around her, holding her so tightly she could hardly breathe.

Tuck bounded toward her, tail wagging. Sara bent down and buried her face in his fur.

When she stood up, Steve motioned her toward the dining room table. "Sit down and tell me everything."

Sara nodded and signed *wait*. Slowly, she took off her coat and hung it in the hall closet. Her insides twisted with apprehension.

In the dining room, Steve was waiting for her, seated at the table with a questioning look on his face. Haltingly, Sara started signing and speaking as Steve watched her intently.

She began with the time she had first tried to slow down on the expressway, and found the brakes weren't working. She went on to describe her near collision with the oil tanker, and the frightening ride off the road.

During her story, Steve sat perfectly still and made no move to interrupt with questions. Sara studied his face, trying to gauge his reaction. His tight-lipped expression told her nothing, but he was upset, and angry. She could feel it radiating from him like heat.

*I knew you shouldn't drive after what happened,* he signed sharply. *There is a dangerous gang operating in Radley right now.* His fingers chopped the air. "*Reports of vandalism. Random violence.*"

Before Sara realized what was happening, Steve leaned forward. He put his face close to hers. "From now on you'll do as I say," he said sharply, and sat back in his chair.

Sara swallowed hard. Her fingers moved. *Violence. Not random,* she signed. *For a reason.*

Sara wanted to pour out the rest of her story but Steve wasn't paying attention anymore. He was looking at the beeper on his belt. Sara realized it must have gone off.

Steve tapped the beeper to stop its signal. He unclipped it from his belt. *That's the hospital. It must be Marisa.*

He went to the phone and punched in the number. Sara watched him closely. She could tell that he was excited by what he heard.

When he hung up the phone, Steve hurried toward her. She read his lips. "Marisa said Charlie Dolan looks like he is regaining consciousness. I've got to get there right now and talk to him. I might not have much time."

Steve threw on his coat and looked at Sara sternly. "You stay right here. I've done enough worrying for one night." His expression softened. "If I find out anything, I'll call you from the TTY at the hospital. I promise."

When he was gone, Sara walked to the window and stared out at the lights of downtown Radley. Somewhere out there was Amy's killer. Was it the same person who had tried to kill her tonight, or was her brake line slashed as part of a sick prank, one of those random acts of violence Steve talked about? In her mind she pictured that blond boy with the lurching walk, then painted a ski mask on his face. Maybe he was the leader of the gang Steve talked about.

Sara sighed. She had finally worked up the

courage to tell Steve everything, and then lost her chance. Somehow, she'd have to try all over again tomorrow. She was surprised to find that she was no longer worried about his anger. The only thing that mattered was giving him the information that could help solve Amy's murder.

Tuck brushed against her leg. Sara leaned down and stroked his ears. She turned from the window and sank down on the couch. Then she kicked her shoes off and lay down on the cushions. She closed her eyes and tried to visualize a quiet beach on a summer night. She tried to imagine she was lying there, instead of all alone in the apartment.

Sara drifted into a fitful sleep. She tossed and turned as images raced through her mind. She was being chased through woods thick with mist, by terrifying, faceless creatures with blazing eyes. She ran and ran, and they never caught her, but were always close behind, so close she could feel their outstretched hands touching her hair.

She awoke with a start, to find the message light blinking on her TTY. She hurried to check it.

While she was asleep, Steve had called. The letters of his message jumped out at her from the screen.

**CHARLIE DOLAN CONFESSED TO AMY HENDERSEN'S MURDER.**

## Chapter 16

Sara was awakened by the flashing light of her alarm. She reached over and turned it off. She felt totally exhausted. Memories of the night before swirled in her head. She remembered Charlie Dolan's confession.

She slid her feet into slippers and yawned. Frown lines creased her forehead. Why would Charlie Dolan have wanted to kill Amy? There was a piece missing from the puzzle.

She had received threats and demands for negatives after Dolan had ended up at the hospital, unconscious. He must have been mixed up with someone else.

Sara pushed her tangled hair from her face and put on a robe. As she padded into the hallway, she saw her brother in the kitchen, pouring a glass of milk. She took a deep breath. Time to face the music.

*Hi,* Steve signed. *You don't look as if you slept well.*

Sara shook her head and signed, *I didn't. We have to talk.*

Steve tapped his chest. *Me first.*

Sara waited impatiently as Steve continued to sign. *Charlie's confession doesn't mean the case is solved. By the time I got to the hospital, he was unconscious again. He only woke up for a few minutes, but he told Marisa that he killed Amy.*

Steve paused for a moment. He tilted his head back, then looked at Sara again and spoke haltingly as she stared at his lips. "When I put Charlie Dolan's name in the computer, I didn't like the information that came out. He used to live in Boston, where he confessed to a total of twenty crimes — including robbery, grand theft auto, and murder."

Sara jumped back in her chair. Steve held up his hand like a stop sign to show that he wasn't finished.

The story unfolded as Sara strained to follow all the words. Steve did his best to sign as much as he could.

After reading the computer report on Dolan, Steve talked with a detective he knew in Boston. Apparently Charlie Dolan was one of those disturbed people who felt guilty and compelled to confess to committing crimes they had nothing to do with. Getting attention was part of it, too. Police departments all across the country were plagued by such people, who insisted on their guilt again and again, tangling in case after case.

Charlie Dolan had gotten therapy before he left Boston, but his psychological problem might have persisted. Perhaps it had resurfaced because of his accident. Steve's conclusion was that Dolan's confession was more likely false than true — though he couldn't be sure. With Dolan still in a coma, things were up in the air.

Steve frowned as he wrapped up the story. Then he looked Sara straight in the eye. "I asked you before if you knew anything about negatives being connected to Amy's murder. Now I'm asking you again."

Sara drew her breath in, and covered her mouth with her hand.

Steve raised his eyebrows. He brushed his index finger across his palm. *What?*

Sara went to the hall closet and took the threatening note from her pocket. She returned to the kitchen and put it in Steve's hand.

As he read, Steve's expression changed from curious, to surprised, to horrified. He flung it on the counter and looked at Sara. His hands sliced angrily through the air. *Why didn't you show me this?*

Sara could feel her face grow hot. *I tried last night. Then you had to leave.*

Steve pursed his lips angrily. *That's no excuse. You should have brought it to me the minute you got it.* His jaw dropped. "This had something to do with your brake line being slashed!" he blurted. Steve grabbed her by the shoulders and gave her a shake so hard that her teeth rattled. "Tell me exactly what is going on. Don't you dare hide anything."

Sara pushed Steve away and began signing quickly, punching her words through the air.

She could feel the vibration of her angry voice in her throat.

*"Don't touch me! You hid things. Tried to say Amy's murder was an accident."* She shot a look at him that was full of venom.

*Stop! Don't argue. Tell me what is going on.*

It took a moment before Sara could begin. She was trembling with anger. Steve waited, his arms folded across his chest, his eyes blazing.

Sara poured out her story, telling him everything from the attack at the library to the incident in the basement of the stationery store. She told him how Mark Royce had demanded some pictures from Amy's notebook and later how she had caught Charlie Dolan going through her locker. She told him about the message Keesha got about the negatives, too. She didn't leave out a single detail.

Although Steve's face grew pale and tight, Sara continued. *I think it all has something to do with pictures of Amy and Wayne Hansen,* she finished. *I have them, and the negatives, in my locker at school.*

Steve looked away. He turned his eyes to

the ceiling. Sara's insides churned as she waited.

*Why, Sara?* he signed. Then he grabbed her arm roughly and spoke into her face. "You withheld information from an investigation. You could have been killed. Do you realize what you have done?"

Sara faced her brother defiantly. *"What else could I do? You lied to me. Threatened me."* She thrust her fingers sharply through the air. *"You said you'd have me followed. Keep me from going to school. It would be like jail."* She put her hands on her hips and stared at her brother, her eyes flashing.

The anger faded from Steve's face. His shoulders sagged. "Maybe it is my fault." He looked at Sara, his eyes filled with sadness. "I just can't do this. Too much responsibility. Maybe you should go back to Edgewood."

Sara felt a tug at her heart. She tapped her index and middle finger quickly against her thumb. *No.* She shook her head, then drew a circle around her heart. *Sorry. Please. I want to stay with you.* She brought her fists together in front of her chest and pointed to Steve.

Her brother shook his head. "I don't know, Sara. I just don't know. I'll have to do a lot of thinking." He rubbed his chin with his hand. "Not now, though. I'm coming to school with you to get those pictures, and those negatives."

At school there was a banner hung over the entrance to the auditorium, announcing that it was the location of the Radley Business Association Scholarship Exam. Sara blinked when she saw it. She had completely forgotten about the exam.

A stream of students went into the auditorium. She studied the looks on their faces. Some smiled eagerly, but most looked worried, and tense. Sara bit her lip. This exam was important to them, she knew. But to her it was insignificant, next to nothing compared to the importance of finding her friend's killer.

Here and there, questioning looks were sent Steve's way. The Radley students who knew he was her brother cast sidelong glances at Sara, silently asking, What's he doing here?

Sara stopped at her locker and spun the combination. It clicked and she opened the door, took out the envelope of photos and handed them to Steve. He flipped quickly through the pictures. Sara could see the wheels turning in his mind, trying to find the key to what made the negatives so important.

He shrugged. "I don't get it, but I'll have to study them some more. I need to get hold of Mark Royce and ask him some questions about these." He waved the photos in the air.

Sara nodded that she understood. She pointed toward the auditorium and signed, *exam.* Together she and her brother joined the line of students filing toward the entrance.

Steve tapped her arm. *"Wait. I see Mark over there."* Sara followed as Steve cut through the crowd toward Mark.

Mark Royce's shoulders swung as he walked. He stared straight ahead. When Steve stepped in front of him he jumped. Sara knew his mind had been focused completely on the exam ahead.

As Steve began talking Mark's tight, tense expression changed to one of annoyance. He kept shaking his head, and glancing from the auditorium entrance to his watch.

Steve refused to hurry. He held the photos with Amy in them in front of Mark's eyes one by one. Mark stiffened and stood up straighter. He jabbed his index finger angrily at Steve's chest.

Steve brushed his hand away. From the way his lips moved and the no-nonsense look on his face, Sara was sure he was speaking sharply to Mark. Students in the hall were eyeing the pair warily.

Mark's going to lose it, Sara thought. She was right. Suddenly, he exploded, flinging the books in his hand on the floor. Everyone nearby jumped back — except Steve. He moved in on Mark, his hands held with palms out in front of his chest, motioning for Mark to take it easy. Mark was too far gone. Sara gasped as he lunged at her brother.

## Chapter 17

Sara stared as Mark grabbed Steve's collar in his huge fists. The crowd that surrounded Mark and Steve moved back, widening the circle around them. They stood gaping at the scene, poised for the fight they were sure would come. They measured the young detective with their eyes, and the same thought formed in everyone's mind. This time Mark Royce would get what was coming to him.

Steve stood his ground and stared Mark dead in the eye. The bones of his tightly clenched jaw jutted against his skin. Still staring Mark in the eye, Steve raised his chin slightly.

Sara dug her nails into her palms. Anger pulsed through her at the sight of Mark's hands on her brother. Her mind was on fire. She had the overwhelming urge to spring at Mark, to knock his hands away.

If Mark hadn't let go of her brother that instant, Sara didn't know what she would have done. But he dropped his hands suddenly, and backed away, his head bowed. He mumbled something Sara couldn't understand. She was sure it was an apology.

Steve's body relaxed. He put his hand on Mark's shoulder and leaned close to him as he talked. The two of them walked a little ways away. The crowd parted to let them pass. A moment later, Mark walked into the auditorium. Steve came back to Sara.

*"You shoudn't have let him go!"* Sara blurted out.

Steve glanced at the students standing around. He took Sara aside, into an empty classroom.

Sara faced him angrily. *"Why didn't you take him away?"*

*"He was all upset about having his chance*

*at the exam ruined. I wouldn't have gotten anything out of him. Let him take his exam. Then he'll go down to the station with me."*

*"You should't have let him go,"* Sara insisted. *"He's mixed up in Amy's murder. I know it."*

Steve touched Sara's cheek. *"He isn't going anywhere."* Sara started to sign, but Steve took her hand in his and held up his other hand for silence. "Not now," he said. He glanced away for a moment, then looked at her solemnly. "You go to class. At the end of the day I'll have an officer waiting in Mr. Morrow's office to take you home. You're grounded until I find out who was behind those threats and attacks . . ." Steve's voice trailed off for a moment. ". . . and until I decide where you're going to live."

Sara started to protest, but Steve stopped her with a glare. "That's final, Sara. I don't want one word from you."

That moment marked the beginning of an even more strained time between Sara and Steve. Day after day went by, unchanging.

Steve dropped Sara off at school in the morning. Lt. Marino escorted her home at the end of the day.

Sara withdrew. For the first time she stayed alone in the apartment and hardly minded. She was too numb.

Sometimes Keesha came over in the afternoon to keep her company. Sara felt as close to her as ever, but even her friend's presence couldn't drive away the hollow feeling inside. She felt that a shadow had settled over her life. She was waiting inside it — waiting to find out who had murdered Amy, and waiting to find out if Steve would send her away.

Meanwhile, Steve questioned Mark about the photos and nothing came of it. He swore he never demanded the negatives, nor had he attacked or threatened Sara. He steadfastly denied having anything to do with Amy's murder.

Steve studied the pictures, examined the negatives, and couldn't find anything that gave him a clue. At East End General, Charlie Dolan remained in a coma. The investigation hung in limbo. Sara felt as if her life did also.

The frightening threats and suspicious incidents stopped abruptly. Sara thought it was because the negatives were no longer in her hands. Steve thought it was because she had a police escort.

Three days after the Radley Business Association's scholarship exam, the winner was announced on the loudspeaker in homeroom. It was a student from Radley Academy, Joel Winters.

For the entire day, little, skinny Joel strutted about with his chest puffed out. He wore his happiness and pride like a banner. Mark Royce showed no reaction, but Sara knew he was devastated. She was surprised that it didn't give her much pleasure.

Where will this all end? she asked herself as she lay on her bed that afternoon, staring at the ceiling. She and Steve were barely talking. When they were together it was as if they performed a tense little dance around each other. She still hadn't heard from Bret, nor did she feel like calling.

Sara heaved herself off the bed and went to her closet. She took out the sweater Amy's mother had given her. She held it in front of her and remembered the last time she had seen Amy wear it. It was the first time they had gotten together to work on the history project. How happy Amy had been then. It seemed years ago instead of weeks.

As she turned to put it back in the closet, Sara ran her hand over the sweater. There was something in the pocket. The sweater was so heavy that she could hardly feel it, but it was there. Sara stuck her fingers inside to see what it was, and pulled out a thin, opaque envelope. She held it in front of her, too dumbstruck to move. *Negatives,* she signed in her thoughts.

Excitement began to surge through Sara's veins. The party photos weren't the negatives that had caused all the trouble. It was the ones she was holding in her hand. For the first time in days, Sara felt alive.

She could hardly get her coat on fast enough. Her car was still in the shop, so Sara got her bike from the storage room downstairs and pedaled toward downtown

Radley. There was a one-hour photo place where she could get the negatives developed right away.

Her heart was racing by the time she pulled in front of the store's yellow door. She looked carefully for Steve as she parked her bike out of sight in an alley.

"I need some film developed right away," she said breathlessly to the clerk behind the counter, a woman with a puffy, teased, red beehive hairdo. "Can you really do it in an hour?"

The woman took a pen from behind her ear. "That's what the sign says," she said, looking as if she had answered the same question too many times. She took the envelope from Sara's hand.

Hurry, Sara thought as she watched the woman label the film and take it to a room in the back. She tapped her foot nervously.

"Go for a walk or something," the woman said when she returned. "You'll be watching the clock if you stay here. Come back at four."

Sara shook her head politely. "I'll wait."

The woman raised her penciled eyebrows that arched above her eyes like wings on her forehead. "Suit yourself." She pursed her lips sourly. "Everyone is always in such a hurry."

Sara hardly paid attention. She was thinking that she would find the clue that would solve Amy's murder. She would take it to Steve and he would bring in the killer. When he realized how she had helped, everything would be put right between them.

Sara fidgeted in her seat. There was so much riding on these negatives. She wanted to be there to get them the moment they were ready.

Just then Sara saw what was one of the few sights that could take her mind off those negatives. Bret Sanderson was coming down the street, looking right through the window at her. Then he was opening the door.

Sara held her breath as Bret came into the shop. He crossed the room in quick, long strides. In a moment he was beside her.

*It's so good to see you,* Sara signed as she looked into his deep brown eyes.

Bret's fingers slowly traced the curve of

her cheek. *"You too, Sara."* He ran his hand along her arm. *I'm sorry I haven't called. I had to sort things out.*

The woman behind the counter had stopped what she was doing and was watching them as if she was looking at a television show. Sara looked at the clock. There were forty-five minutes left before the film would be ready. She stood up. "I'll come back at four o'clock," she said. As she left, the woman looked even more disgruntled than when she had said she would stay.

*Tell me how you've been,* Sara signed to Bret as they walked. Now that she was with him, she realized that she had missed him even more than she thought.

*All right. Not great, frankly. Like I said, I had to sort things out.*

Sara stopped in front of him and studied his face. *And . . . ?*

Bret took her in his arms and held her. Their lips met in a long kiss.

*I love you, Sara,* Bret signed. *I suppose I knew it all along. Let's meet each other halfway. Before you get involved in some-*

*thing dangerous, think of me. If you decide you have to go ahead, I'll try to live with it — try hard. Promise me you'll try just as hard to be careful.*

*I promise.* Sara's heart soared. She looked into Bret's eyes. *I love you, too.*

The minutes flew by for Sara and Bret. Three quarters of an hour was gone in a breath as they tried to catch up on everything. Bret was true to his word. He listened to Sara tell him everything that she had done to involve herself in the investigation without objecting or getting angry.

When Sara glanced at the clock above the entrance to the bank, she was shocked. *It's five minutes after four!* She turned to go.

*I'm coming with you,* Bret signed. *If there is something that's going to wrap up this investigation, and your part in it, I want to be there to see it.*

Together they hurried back to the photo store.

The red-haired clerk raised her penciled eyebrows as she handed Sara the envelope. "I don't know what you were in such a hurry for," she said with a smirk. "Only four pictures came out and there's nothing but a bunch of little dots in any of them."

Sara's throat tightened. The clerk watched with suspicious curiosity as Bret signed to Sara. *She takes lots of interest in her work.*

Sara was too nervous to appreciate his tart humor. Her fingers trembled as she opened the envelope.

She frowned as she looked at the photos. The clerk was giving her a look that said, "I told you so." She pushed the bill toward Sara.

"Wait a minute." Sara waved it away. "Do you have a magnifying glass?"

The clerk tapped her pen on the counter to indicate that she thought her valuable time was being wasted. She reached under the counter and came out with a magnifying glass, handing it to Sara as if performing a special favor.

Sara held the glass over the photos one by one. At first they still looked like page after page covered with random patterns of dots. Then suddenly, she read the words at the top of each photo, and everything snapped into focus. She had been too wrapped up in the murder investigation to take much of an interest in the Radley Business Association Scholarship Exam. Now she understood that it was behind everything that had happened recently. In her hand were pictures of the exam answer sheets!

*Chapter 18*

The next morning students in home-rooms all over Radley were stunned by the news that the results of the Radley Business Association Scholarship Exam were being thrown out. Principals and school heads read from the Association's official statement, which said that the members reasoned they had no way of knowing if any of the competitors had seen the answers.

Joel Winters was in Sara's homeroom. When he heard the news his small form seemed to shrink in size. A moment later he jumped from his chair and bolted into the hall, his hand held over his mouth as if he was going to be sick.

Sara glared at Mark Royce, who sat on the

other side of the classroom. It's all your fault, she thought.

Mark turned and stared back at her, his face devoid of expression. His eyes were as empty as cubes of ice.

That day, Sara didn't eat lunch in the cafeteria with Keesha and Liz. She went to the Radley Academy Library and stared out the window. She wanted to be alone.

Amy's murder wasn't the only thing on her mind. Steve told her to come to his office at the precinct after school so they could talk. She was afraid of what he was going to say.

That afternoon, Sara's feet dragged as she went up the steps of the precinct to Steve's office on the second floor. All day long she kept asking herself the same question. What will I do if he wants to send me away?

She had loved being at Edgewood, loved being part of a deaf community. But it couldn't take the place of being with the only family she had left.

Steve was sitting behind his desk with his hands folded when Sara arrived. He motioned for her to sit down, and then closed the door.

They faced each other across the desk. Don't send me away, Sara told him with her eyes.

*I've been doing a lot of thinking*, Steve signed. Sara could see that he was trying very hard to get every word exactly right. Her breath lodged in her throat.

*It has been wonderful having you here, but it has been hard, too.* Steve paused for a moment and touched Sara's hand gently before going on. *It has been hard for both of us.*

Steve looked away for a moment, as if he was considering his words carefully. *I feel I have to do everything right, all the time, and I can't.*

Sara nodded. Her heart felt like lead.

Steve's fingers jabbed the air. *Don't worry. I'm not going to send you back to Edgewood.*

Sara let her breath out in an explosive burst. She jumped from her chair, leaned across the desk to fling her arms around her brother.

Steve drew back. *Wait a minute. I'm not finished.*

Smiling, Sara took her seat. Great waves of relief were washing over her.

*I realize I couldn't expect you not to want to get involved when something happened to a close friend of yours.* Steve raked a hand through his hair. *But I have to keep you safe.* He looked into her eyes. *I need your help, Sara. I can't be your jailer. You'll have to think for yourself, keep yourself out of danger. Not hide things from me. No more playing detective.*

Sara knew Steve wanted her to promise. She swallowed. She wasn't sure it was a promise she could keep. He was staring steadily at her. *All right,* she signed.

Steve pressed his lips together. *You'll remember what I said.* He looked at her sternly.

*Yes. Yes I will,* she signed hurriedly.

Steve slapped the desk lightly. *All right, then. I have to get back to work.* He stood up and fished something out of his pocket. "By the way, I picked up your car today. It's parked around the side of the building."

Sara's face beamed as she took the keys. She kissed her brother on the cheek as she left.

Steve watched out the window as Sara crossed the street and got into the green sedan. He hoped he had done the right thing. He wasn't too confident that Sara would stop meddling in his work. He'd just have to deal with the problems as they came. The truth was, he couldn't bring himself to send her away.

Sara felt lightheaded with relief as she pulled onto the road. Her brother had tried hard to understand her and had treated her like an adult. She felt that what had happened had brought them closer together.

So many things had fallen into place for her — she and Bret were back together. Steve hadn't sent her away. And yet with Amy's killer still on the loose, she had the feeling that her own life was on hold.

Sara turned left onto the road that led to the Shadow Point Marina and pressed down on the gas pedal. Trees, stores, used-car lots, and houses flew by. Suddenly she couldn't wait to be near the water. The sight of it always made her feel calmer and more peaceful inside.

On the way to the marina Sara passed the

empty picnic tables in Shadow Point Park. The area around the marina was deserted. Sara didn't care. She liked the stillness.

She parked the car near the closed Boathouse Café and zipped up her jacket. She pulled an extra scarf from the seat behind her and wrapped it around her neck. It would be colder out here on the water.

Not a soul was around as Sara walked past the boats that rocked in the water. In the summer the sky would have been filled with birds. Now nothing broke the chilly gray surface.

Sara clapped her hands together and stepped onto the wooden dock. Her breath blew from her mouth in white clouds.

She walked down the entire length of the dock to the end. A breeze rippled the waves. The water was the same cold shade of gray as the sky. Sara stood looking out at it, hypnotized by its movement.

It wasn't long before Sara could feel the chill seeping into her bones. Winter has lasted much too long, she said to herself.

The thought sent a strange tingle through her. Winter. In her mind she visualized the letters. What was it about that word? She had seen it on a sign on her way to the marina, and hardly noticed it. Not winter, Winters.

Her mind exploded with light. She had driven past the Winters Used Car lot dozens of times, but hadn't paid any attention to the sign. Now she remembered that it belonged to Joel Winters' father. Joel complained now and then because his father made him help out there.

The car that had chased her that night belonged to a used car lot. She was willing to bet the lot was owned by Joel's father.

She wasn't sure how the boys in the ski masks tied into the whole story, and she wasn't going to wait to figure it out. She had to get to Steve.

Sara whirled around to run back to her car. Instead, she ran right into Joel Winters.

She didn't have to look twice to know that Joel wasn't in his right mind. His eyes had an eerie shine and his mouth was twisted into something between a smile and a sneer. He took a deep breath and moved toward her. "You ruined everything," he said.

Sara took a step backwards, glancing over

her shoulder at the edge of the dock. There wasn't much room behind her. Fear pulsed through her in a nauseous wave. She turned to face Joel.

"I had that scholarship right in my hands. Then you had to spoil it."

"I didn't do it to hurt you," Sara said. Her eyes darted right and left. Normally she would have risked going hand to hand with Joel. She was still in good shape from crew practice, and Joel was very small, and looked as if he never did anything more physical than punch a calculator.

Now, however, Joel seemed frenzied. She had heard how strong someone who was out of his mind could be.

Sara weighed her chances. She had to do something fast. Whatever Joel was planning wasn't going to be good for her.

Sara took a step forward and prepared to run. She was going to try to race past him and get to her car.

She and Joel looked at each other and their eyes locked. In Joel's eyes she saw the depths of something that was beyond reason. He shook his head slowly, and one side of his lip curled.

"Uh-uh-uh," he said, waving his index finger at her. "Don't even try it." Then he sprang toward her.

Sara leaped backwards, with no thought of how dangerously close to the edge of the dock she was. Joel sprang toward her again, his hands reaching out for her.

Sara threw her arms in front of her face and leaped backwards once more. For an instant she felt the crumbling edge of the dock underneath the toes of her boots. She teetered precariously on the edge, then started to free-fall into the freezing waters below.

## Chapter 19

Sara felt Joel crushing the ends of her fingers in his grasp as he yanked her forward at the last minute. He pulled her roughly back onto the dock and threw her down.

Sara pushed herself up and bolted away from him. She stumbled forward and nearly fell, but regained her balance and ran again. Joel caught her coat collar and spun her around. "Not so fast," he said. "I have a few things to tell you." He pushed her toward the edge of the dock and stood in front of her. "Don't move."

Sara gulped in air, and felt perspiration trickling down her neck. She wished she didn't have to look at Joel's face — to see the terrifying, maniacal gleam in those eyes. But she didn't dare take her eyes off him for a second.

"Everything was turning out perfectly." Sara watched Joel's lips moving. "Then you had to start poking around, poking around, poking around. You just wouldn't stop. Now I'll have to stop you."

"I didn't think you would lose the scholarship," Sara said hurriedly.

Joel cupped his hand behind his ear. "Did I hear you say you didn't think?" His lip curled into a sneer. "You ruined my life, and all because you didn't think!"

"You're smart, Joel. You can still go to college."

Joel shook his head slowly. "You just don't get it, do you? My father doesn't want me to go to college. He wants me to help him run that stupid used car lot. If I want to go I have to have all expenses paid. All of them. This was the only one that did that."

Sara struggled not to show her fear. "You could get a job to pay some of the cost," she said.

That was a mistake. Joel stamped his foot angrily and bent over and leaned close. "No, no, no!" he screamed. Sara could tell because of the way his mouth twisted. "That's not the way I want it — struggling along, no time to myself. I deserve better. I'm too smart for that!"

Keep him talking, Sara thought desperately. Keep him talking and pray you'll find a way out of this. "You're right, Joel. You're smart. You're very smart."

Joel threw back his head and laughed. "I can see those wheels turning in your head." He twirled his index finger beside his temple. "You want to keep me talking. Well, okay. Let's talk. Somebody might as well know everything I went through to win that scholarship. Especially since you won't be around to tell anyone else."

Sara's blood froze. In the back of her mind, she had known he was planning to kill her. Her mouth felt dry.

Joel began rambling. Sara couldn't read all of the torrent of words that poured from his lips, but she knew enough to piece together the chilling tale.

He had used his father's credit card to ob-

tain the cash he needed to bribe Charlie
Dolan to unlock the file cabinet that held the
answer sheets for the scholarship exam.
Charlie didn't want to risk being caught
using the copy machine, so he snapped photos of the answers. Joel arranged to pay him
when he got the developed photos, and the
negatives.

He met Charlie in the hall the next day
after school was over. Charlie had just
handed over everything, when Amy Hendersen came along.

Sara gasped. That must have been the day
Amy had gone back to get her history project
notebook. She remembered how distracted
she had been afterwards.

"It was the first in a series of bad breaks,"
Joel said. "Amy didn't want things messed
up for her precious Mark. She threatened to
tell if I didn't give the photos and the negatives to her. She ripped up the photos into
tiny pieces and threw them in the garbage.
She stuffed the negatives in a flap in the back
of her notebook."

Joel's face reddened with rage as he explained how hard he had tried to put the pieces of the photos back together, but it had been impossible. Charlie Dolan had refused to risk taking any more pictures if he didn't get more money.

From that moment on, Joel had watched Amy's every move. When Sara dropped her off at the library, he went inside and told her they needed to talk. He managed to persuade her to go outside.

That's when things got ugly. Amy refused to give up the film, even when Joel offered her five hundred dollars. They struggled, and the last time he pushed her, she hit her head on the brick wall of the library, and fell to the ground.

"I couldn't believe she was dead," Joel's face went slack and dull for a moment. His eyes lit up again and he said, horribly, "But I didn't care. All I worried about was that someone would remember seeing me talk to her in the library. If her body was found there, the police would come straight to me. I had to get the body away from there." Joel pulled his lips back from his teeth in an eerie grin. "That's when I had a real stroke of genius."

Sara stood there, paralyzed with shock as Joel unfolded the rest of his terrible tale. He had pulled his car around to the dark, narrow street behind the library and dragged Amy's body inside. He had taken her to Shadow Point Park, left the body near the pond, and called Mark Royce. "He was so jealous he fell for my story about Amy meeting Wayne just like that," Joel snapped his fingers. "It was perfect. I killed two birds with one stone," Joel laughed at his sick joke. "Now it's your turn."

Sara held her breath. Joel looked at her and smiled his eerie smile. "I'm not ready to kill you yet," he said. "I think you ought to know just how perfectly I figured everything out."

Sara nodded, her hand on her stomach. As long as Joel kept talking, she still had a chance. "What about the guys in the ski masks?" She managed to get the words out.

Joel tapped his forehead with his index finger. "I knew I couldn't be seen doing anything suspicious." Joel shrugged his skinny shoulders. "So I hired Bobby Neenan to do my dirty work for me. He recruited some of his pals who like to cause trouble just for fun. He even got his ten-year-old brother to grab that envelope from the newsstand."

Joel sighed. "It cost money, though. More and more money, and I still didn't get my negatives. You just wouldn't cooperate."

Joel's shoulders sagged. "The worst part is that I won after all, fair and square, without the answers. I won, and then I lost." A bubble of crazy laughter escaped Joel's lips, then another and another. His whole body shook with laughter he couldn't seem to stop.

Sara recognized her only chance and took it. She shoved past Joel and raced down the dock. She had only taken a few steps when she felt his hand grab the back of her collar. He caught her and pushed her roughly, once, twice. Fueled with rage, Joel gave one last powerful push and sent Sara over the edge.

As Sara felt the icy water engulf her she reached out and caught Joel by the ankle. His foot shot out as he tried to kick her away.

Then Joel, too, tumbled into the Buckeye River.

They thrashed about in the piercing, wet cold. Joel managed to get his hands around Sara's neck. She coughed and fought for air, striking out with her fists, hitting Joel wherever she could, as hard as she could.

The freezing water closed over her head, but she managed to resurface, gasping for air. She was fighting for survival, her own adrenaline racing now, pumping through her veins.

Sara was in much better shape than Joel. Hours of crew practice had hardened the muscles of her arms. As they continued to fight, her natural advantage began to prevail.

Sara twisted and jabbed her elbow into Joel's ribs. The impact caught Joel by surprise. His grip on Sara's neck loosened for a moment and Sara surged through the water. She turned and swam for the dock with every ounce of strength left in her.

Each furious stroke took her farther away from Joel. Though her coat was saturated with water and so heavy it dragged her down, she managed to make it to the dock. In a final burst of strength, she pulled herself out of the water.

As Sara collapsed on the dock, her eyes searched the water for Joel. There was nothing visible on the surface of the choppy gray river. Joel was gone.

# Chapter 20

A thin hand shot through the water. Then Joel's head bobbed to the surface. His mouth was open, and his face was contorted with terror. His head sank down under the water again. For a moment Sara couldn't see him. Then he rose above the water. She saw his arms thrashing before he went down once more.

Joel burst through the water and sank again before Sara realized he was drowning. Sara's eyes searched wildly, looking for someone to help. The area was as deserted as it had been when she drove up. The realization that she would have to save the person who had just tried to kill her crackled through her.

Sara's brain shifted into automatic. She performed every action almost without thinking, propelled only by the knowledge of what had to be done.

In a single motion she stripped off her coat and shot into the water. As her arms sliced through the freezing river, she no longer felt the cold. She reached Joel in seconds.

Joel had been overtaken by panic and struck out at Sara, hitting her in the jaw. But he was so weak at that point that there was hardly any force behind it.

Sara pushed Joel out in front of her and grabbed him from behind. She swirled around in the water, her legs pumping hard all the way back to the dock. She pulled them both to safety.

When Joel's body lay on the dock, Sara pushed the heels of her hands into his chest below the rib cage, once, twice. He gurgled, and a thin stream of water poured from his lips. A fit of coughing seized him.

Sara didn't wait another second before she jumped to her feet. Her boots thudded over the cold, hard ground as she raced to her car. On her portable TTY she reached Steve at his office. **EMERGENCY, LIFE AND DEATH. GET AMBULANCE,** she typed urgently, and described her location.

It was only when she signed off, and cast an anxious look down the dock and saw Joel lying there, that feeling rushed back into her body. She began shivering so hard that her teeth rattled as they knocked together. She switched on the heat and huddled in her car, praying that Steve would come soon.

It seemed that hours passed as Sara waited, though actually only minutes went by. Finally she saw the welcome sight of the ambulance's flashing lights. She jumped out of the car as she saw the police cruiser behind it. Tears of relief flowed down her face as it pulled to a stop and Steve got out. She ran to him and threw her arms around his neck in a thankful embrace.

In the weeks that followed, Bobby Neenan and his gang of thugs were arrested. At East End General Hospital, Charlie Dolan regained consciousness and confessed once more to the murder of Amy Hendersen. This time, however, a long conversation with a

staff psychiatrist revealed that what moti-
vated his confession was guilt over his part in
the events leading to the murder, rather than
guilt over the actual crime.

"Dolan will probably get off with paying a
heavy fine for stealing those exam scores,"
Steve told Sara. "But I think he'll suffer re-
morse over Amy's murder for the rest of his
life."

Sara thought Steve was right. She thought
Joel would suffer, too. He had been commit-
ted to a psychiatric facility, and would re-
main there for a long, long time.

After Joel had been caught, Steve had
gone to his home and visited his room — a
room that his parents had not entered for several months. There he had a frightening
glimpse into the private world of Joel Winters.

In a kind of wild, rambling diary scrawled
on a dozen lined paper pads, Joel had revealed his seething rage at almost everyone —
his parents, his fellow students — and partic-
ularly Amy Hendersen and Sara Howell. He
had even tacked up newspaper pictures of
Sara on the crew team and slashed angrily

across them in red ink. It was shocking how well he had managed to hide the depth of his disturbance.

In a strange way, one person benefited from what happened, though in losing Amy he lost far more than he gained. The Radley Business Association put together another scholarship exam. The winner was Mark Royce.

Two days after winning, however, Mark surprised everyone by rejecting the award. He said he couldn't live with himself if he kept it, after what had happened to his girlfriend. The scholarship went to the person who had scored second highest on the exam, Karen Lee.

*Epilogue*

A month had passed since Amy's death. One late afternoon as the sun barely filtered through the cold gray clouds, Sara knelt to put fresh flowers on her father's grave. She said a silent good-bye to him, and walked along the row of graves, past headstone after headstone, toward the pale pink marble marker where Amy was buried.

I'm sorry I haven't been able to visit your grave before, she whispered to Amy with her heart. I just couldn't bring myself to do it. But I've thought about you every day.

As Sara neared the grave site she stopped suddenly, riveted by what she saw. A boy was bending over the grave. His fingers touched the headstone and stroked the marble surface as gently as if he were caressing a loved one's face. He was Mark Royce — a very different Mark Royce from the one Sara had known.

On bended knee, Mark set down a huge bouquet of roses. His large hand undid the satin ribbon that bound them together, and he spread them all over the ground, until they covered Amy's grave with their colors — deep red, pale yellow, pink and white.

He got to his feet and stood still and straight, a solitary figure outlined against the sky. He stood with his head bowed and his hands clasped in front of him for a while. Then his fingers brushed the headstone in another soft caress.

For a moment Sara stood watching, hypnotized by the tender feeling that flowed from Mark. Then she turned her face away. What was happening should be between him and Amy.

Sara returned to the car, where Steve and Bret were waiting for her. *I'll visit Amy's grave another time*, she signed, and sank back into the seat. Steve and Bret didn't ask any questions. Without a word, Steve began driving. The three of them were lost in their thoughts.

After twenty minutes, Steve pulled in front of the Side Door Café. "We all need a lift," he said, "and I think this is the place to get it."

Sara realized that she couldn't have agreed more. Once they were seated in a booth in the cheery, bustling café, the heaviness of her mood began to subside.

The waitress brought three cappuccinos and three hot, fragrant slices of apple pie. Sara reached for her fork, but Bret put his hand over hers and then signed, *Wait. Steve and I have been wanting to tell you something.*

Sara raised her eyebrows questioningly.

*No more meddling in my cases,* Steve signed slowly.

*No more playing detective,* Bret's fingers moved quickly. He looked at her sternly.

Steve began signing again. *No more worrying us both to death. I mean it. Promise.*

The two of them stared at her expectantly, waiting for her promise.

Sara rested her hands on the table. She had been wondering when this confrontation would come, and had thought long and hard about how she would respond. She waited a moment before replying, forming her thoughts carefully. Then she signed and spoke to them.

*"I'll try, but I can't give you my promise, since I'm not sure I could keep it. I don't mean to worry you. I love you both."* She spread her hands helplessly. *"But what drives me to do what I do is part of who I am. I am a detective's daughter, and a detective's sister."*

Steve and Bret exchanged glances. They both looked at Sara with resignation. Bret squeezed her hand gently.

Keesha appeared beside the booth. "Hi. Want some company?" she asked brightly.

Sara motioned for her to sit down. The waitress brought another cappuccino and a piece of apple pie for Keesha. Soon they were all talking and laughing together.

As the four of them left the café, Sara

knew that she would never forget her friend Amy, and that she would always have a special place in her heart. She would always hold her close, but she would find a way to keep her memories, and still move on. It was time to begin a new chapter in her life.

Every day

*Sara Howell*

faces mystery, danger ... and silence.

# Will Sara go from being a hero to being dead?

Radley's reeling from a string of fires—that the
authorities think is arson! The only good news is
that a little boy is still alive after being rescued
from the flames—by Sara! The town makes her a
hero, but the arsonist vows to get even. Will Sara
be the arsonist's next target?

# HEAR NO EVIL #6
## Playing with Fire

### Kate Chester

Coming soon to a bookstore near you.

# Their lives are nonstop action, inside the hospital and out...

## MED CENTER

Order now...
get in on
the action!

| | | | |
|---|---|---|---|
| BBX54322-9 | #1 *Virus* | $3.99 | ☐ |
| BBX54323-7 | #2 *Flood* | $3.99 | ☐ |
| BBX67316-5 | #3 *Fire* | $3.99 | ☐ |
| BBX67317-3 | #4 *Blast* | $3.99 | ☐ |

**Available wherever you buy books, or use this order form.**
Scholastic Inc., P.O. Box 7502, 2931 E. McCarty Street, Jefferson City, MO 65102
Please send me the books I have checked above. I am enclosing $_____
(please add $2.00 to cover shipping and handling).
Send check or money order – no cash or C.O.D.s please.

Name_____Birthdate_____

Address _____

City_____ State /Zip_____

Please allow four to six weeks for delivery. Offer good in U.S.A. only. Sorry, mail orders
are not available to residents of Canada. Prices subject to change.                    MC596